The Queens of Time

The Queens of Heaven
Book 2

Andrew S. French

Neonoir Books

Also by Andrew S. French

Science Fiction

The Time Traveller's Murder

The Mercy Sleep

Bodies

The Arcane Supernatural Thriller Series

Book one: The Arcane

Book two: The Arcane Identity

Book three: The Arcane Quest

Book four: The Arcane Ultimatum

The Ella Finn Fantasy Novella Series

Ella and the Elementals

Ella and the Multiverse

Ella and the Monsters

Ella and the Dreamers

Supernatural Short Stories

Dead Souls

Dead Souls II

The Shadow

Writing as A. S. French

Crime Fiction and Thrillers

The Astrid Snow series

Book one: Don't Fear the Reaper

Book two: The Killing Moon

Book three: Lost in America

Book four: Gone to Texas

Book five: The Final Girl

The Ophelia Red series

Book one: Ophelia Red

The Detective Jen Flowers series

Book one: The Hashtag Killer

Book two: Serial Killer

Book three: Night Killer

Book four: The Killer Inside Them

The Frank Walker series

Where The Bodies Are Buried

Bodies of Evidence

Crime Short Stories

Crime Stories: A Collection

Call Me: An Astrid Snow Short Story

Dark Snow: An Astrid Snow Short Story

Bette Davis Eyes: Detective Flowers Short Story

Go to www.andrewsfrench.com for more information.

Chapter 1

London Calling

It was cold at seven fifty-five on an October evening in London and seemed colder as I waited for death from the sky. German bombers were about to lay waste to the land, silently hiding somewhere beyond those marshmallow puffs. But that wasn't why I was there. I'd travelled nearly a hundred years back to 1940, searching for one missing woman to help me find a second missing one.

Blackout conditions were in force. All the windows and doors were covered with heavy curtains, cardboard or paint to prevent the escape of any glimmer of light that might aid enemy aircraft. Darkness shrouded the city, but the moonlight showed me that Balham Underground Station was only a hundred yards away. It was my first trip to this period, but I knew what would happen in a few minutes. All I'd seen of it before was in black and white photographs, newsreels and movie versions, and those images of the first woman I searched for: Ursula. Her face was imprinted onto my memory, as was the location.

I scanned the area, surprised to see people on the street, even at this time of night, with regular German bombardments for over a year. They wouldn't allow the risks to infringe on their lives, but they were oblivious to the imminent death on its way, navigating the dark streets with the help of torches or flashlights covered with red cellophane.

There were only ninety seconds left before the bombs hit, but I was supposed to do nothing. The First Rule of Time: Never interfere with history. Never alter; only watch and record. If any rule was made to be broken, that was it.

'You only observe history, Ruby; you never change it.' Those were the words of my friend and mentor, Diana, the second woman I searched for. She was a Watcher, the people she'd helped me escape from. A debt I had to repay by finding her. And I had to warn those on the street about what was coming.

I gripped the gas mask in my hand and peered through the gloom, seeing the pinpoints of light and bodies moving inside a thick mist. Not only did I have to warn them about the approaching German planes, but I would have to convince them not to go to the shelter in the station.

I stepped out of the doorway, put my fingers to my lips, and whistled as loud as possible. The shapes in the shadows stopped, about a dozen or more of them, and turned to me. The air was heavy with the smell of dampness as the fog blanket separated, and I saw their faces: a woman, her hands shaking, kept glancing into the sky as if she knew what was coming. Her eyes were wide, and her skin was pale as if she'd seen her own ghost. A man beside her was biting his lower lip, and his eyes fixed on me. With a furrowed brow and clenched jaw, it was as if he was bracing himself for bad news. Another woman, her hair pulled back tightly in a bun, stared beyond me. Her face was expressionless, but her eyes betrayed her fear, darting everywhere as if searching for an escape.

Then a child stepped forward and pointed at me. 'Look at that strange woman, Mommy.'

I slapped the gas mask. 'Shit!'

A woman clamped a hand over her mouth while her two children giggled at my choice of language. I gazed at their 1940s clothes and knew why I stood out like a sore thumb. I was still wearing my twenty-first-century gear: tight jeans and a red jacket. They must have thought I was a Nazi spy. The men gazed at me, grim faces battered by the world around them, while the women shielded their children from the stranger in their midst.

There was only a minute to go.

I couldn't return to the base to change clothes and return immediately – the proximity of the time jumps would fire shooting pain through every part of me, and I'd be no use to anybody. And I couldn't send Dash in my place – if the locals were suspicious of me and my attire, they'd freak out on seeing a six-foot-tall walking and talking cat.

No, I was stuck with the consequences of my reckless rush to Balham as the air-raid sirens began their awful, mournful wail.

Her face drained of colour, one woman clutched her

young child to her chest. 'Come on,' she said, her voice trembling. 'We have to get to the shelter.'

A man next to her nodded, his face grim. 'Hurry,' he said, grabbing the hand of a young boy and pulling him along.

Another woman, her eyes filled with tears, frantically searched for someone. 'Has anyone seen my husband?' she cried out, her voice filled with desperation.

A man scanned the sky, trying to stay calm. 'We need to stay together,' he said, his voice steady. 'We'll be safe in the shelter.'

But they wouldn't. Only death waited for them there.

The people scattered and headed for Balham Underground. I stepped into the street and threw the gas mask to the ground to make as much noise as possible. They turned and looked at me.

'Take cover; the bombs are coming.' My eyes bulged, and my lips grew large, my voice as high as possible without tearing my vocal cords from my throat. 'Don't use the Underground.'

History told me death awaited those who went there. A fourteen hundred kilo semi-armour piercing bomb would penetrate thirty-two feet underground and explode above the cross passage between the two platforms. The water main would burst, the flood rolling down the tunnels, right up and down the line, plunging thousands into darkness and water. They would be trapped, struggling, and panicking in the rising black invisible waters. They'd go to the station for safety, only to find something worse than bombs, stepping into an unknown terror: women and children, tiny babes in arms, locked beneath the ground. I could only visualise their horror, only recall what I'd read, but it must have been hell. On top of this would come a cloud of gas. Those not killed outright would suffocate; the rest drowned like rats in a cage.

But I couldn't tell them all that. There wasn't time. The child who had pointed at my strange clothes offered me her hand.

'You better come with us, lady.'

Instinct should have told them to leave, but hardly any of them moved, startled by the crazed young woman telling them not to go where they thought they'd find protection. So instead, everybody else turned their heads to the sky as the sounds of the creeping Luftwaffe approached. A young boy, his eyes wide with fear, was clinging to his mother's leg, his face buried in her dress. Then they heard it.

'Planes!' someone screamed.

I had to save them, had to stop them from going underground. So I ran in front of them and waved my arms. Then I bellowed as loud as possible.

'Run to your homes, anywhere, but not the Underground.'

I was a shrieking banshee, but I don't think they heard me. They scattered like pins downed in a bowling lane, heading in every direction, with no rhyme or reason to where they went, possessed by the human desire to survive. I couldn't stop those who rushed for the station. My heart sank, but I could do nothing for them. I had other priorities.

Focus. I had to focus on why I was there.

My head swivelled to search for Ursula and found nothing.

Did we get the date wrong? Did Gideon lie?

People ran everywhere, diving into alleys and falling into doorways. Chaos and panic ensued apart from one spot: the little kid staring at me from the middle of the road, oblivious to the double-decker bus heading towards her.

The dead air swirled inside my lungs as I sprinted for the girl. The planes were above me, great lumbering shadows ready to thrust their death onto us. The bus steamed forward, desperate to get ahead of the impending doom. I grabbed the girl and threw us both to the ground. The bus missed by inches, the wind from its passing whipping our hair and clothes. My heart pounded as I looked at the bus, its driver not even glancing in our direction. It disappeared from view as the kid clutched to me, her breath warm on my face.

'Are you okay?' I said to her.

The sound of death hung in the air, getting closer by the second. The girl's face was unmoving as she clung to me like a second skin. She didn't speak, instead pointing over my shoulder. I turned to see a shimmering light opposite, and then Ursula appeared on the pavement, maybe fifty feet away, standing below a shop's overhanging canvas. I heard the dropping of the bombs as I shouted to Ursula.

'Move!'

But my voice was obscured by the wail of the explosives around us. Buildings disappeared in vast clouds of smoke and dust as great holes appeared in the road. I watched in despair as the pole connecting the canvas above the shop shattered in one go. It dropped as I shouted again. Only it didn't hit the ground. Instead, it landed on Ursula's head and knocked her to the pavement. I buried the kid's face in my chest, pushed my body into the concrete, and then closed my eyes to the surrounding debris, a tsunami constructed of steel, bricks, and wood. The girl hung onto me as the apocalypse exploded inside my skull.

More explosions shattered the air above us as I pressed the kid underneath me, sheltering her from the storm cloud that swept over everything. The dust invaded my mouth

6

and ears, clogging my lungs as I refused to move. Eventually, I twisted my neck to the side and coughed up my guts but still covered the girl on the ground.

I don't know how long we lay there, but there was confusion everywhere when I lifted my head. The kid was safe and whispered something to me. Only she wasn't whispering; her lips were large and moved at a thousand miles a second, her eyes wide and excitable. She shouted, but I couldn't hear anything apart from the ringing of a million bells in my skull. Finally, I climbed off the girl and gave her some air. Thick grime clung to my lungs as smoke invaded my head, smelling like the middle of a furnace. A few feet away, the dead eyes of the gas mask stared at me. Dense grey dust floated far and wide, creating a blanket of mist obscuring my vision, apart from a few feet ahead. The kid grabbed my arm, shaking me hard. Tiny scraps of sound slithered through my ears, people screaming and shouting, calling out in pain, crying for those lost.

I stood and held the kid's hand. 'Are your parents here?'

My voice sounded as if it was underwater, with lead weights strapped to my legs. Then, something bumped into me, knocking me to one side, and my fingers slipped from the girl. I reached for the gun inside my jacket.

Maybe the Static was already there. Perhaps the girl had been part of their plan to distract me. Confusion overwhelmed my thoughts. A terrified woman covered in dust and bits of debris swept the kid up in her arms, and I guessed mother and daughter were reunited again. I slumped to the ground. My fingers trembled as I pointed the weapon into the chaos surrounding me and searched for enemies that weren't there.

The woman helped me up. 'We have to get to the Underground.'

She wanted to drag me there as I watched the planes heading in that direction.

I shook my head. 'No, it's too dangerous in there. Find shelter somewhere else.'

She didn't reply, but I hoped she'd understood. The girl beamed at me as they moved away. Amongst all the devastation, I saw the love between those two people, and it warmed my heart. And it made me think of my mother. All these years, I'd blamed my parents for abandoning me, for giving me to Diana and the Watchers, but that memory was a lie planted in my head. Put there by Diana, the woman who had become more than a mother to me. As death and destruction fell from the sky, I thought about my mother and father and wondered if they'd loved me in those first fourteen years of my life. After all this time, perhaps I'd been wrong to hate them.

The screeching of sirens kicked me from my reverie, ambulances and fire engines reacting to the bombing. I pushed my fingers into the cold concrete and pressed myself upwards, the swirl of mist dissipating as a gust of wind washed across the street.

Then I remembered why I was there.

'Ursula,' I said as I stumbled to where I'd seen her last.

My foot got caught in some rubble, bringing me crashing down again, and my shoulder smashed into the pavement. Ripples of agony shot down that side of me. Lethargy pounced on my bones. All I wanted to do was lay there and rest. I should have left, gone to the base, recuperated, and returned four minutes later. That would be enough distance in time to allow my body to breathe. It would have been the sensible thing to do.

But I didn't.

I rolled onto my side and stared at Ursula's unconscious

body. Her feet stuck out from beneath the pole that had struck her. She was alive; I knew that from Gideon's bragging in the future. There was no need to stay there and suffer; such are the joys of time travel. But I was sick of running. I moved back onto my stomach. Ursula's feet had disappeared. Different feet crunched through the rubble as I lay there, alarmed at the people who drifted out of the shadows and lifted Ursula off the ground.

The Static.

If it wasn't them, it was somebody who worked for them.

I crawled over broken glass and shattered stones before I got up, my gaze fixed on them as they dragged her towards an ambulance. Every inch of me ached as if that bus had hit me and then ran over me several times. But I had to stop them. I fumbled in my pocket for the laser gun, but all I found was dirt and rubble. I cursed under my breath as I ran at them, my legs moving as if a drunken marionette controlled me. The nearest bloke turned to me as I reached him. He removed one hand from Ursula but wasn't quick enough to stop me. I punched him in the gut, and he let go of Ursula and fell into the ambulance.

'Shoot her,' somebody shouted from the side of the vehicle. The other goon dropped Ursula and reached inside his jacket. I swivelled my hip and kicked him in the knee, sending him into the dust cloud travelling towards us. I heard the bombs hitting more buildings nearby, picturing the destruction happening in Balham Station.

The screaming in my head wasn't only mine as the smoke from the bombing covered me. I took a deep breath as one of them jumped onto my back. We crashed to the ground together and landed near Ursula's unconscious frame. My fingers touched hers as my attacker pulled my hair. He nearly tore the roots from my scalp as I screamed inside my skull, waiting for my head to come off. It didn't, so I threw my elbow back and hit him in the ribs. He let go and tumbled out of sight into the swirling soot and dust that coated everything. I couldn't see Ursula or the ambulance anymore as I took a deep breath and coughed.

Then the sound of gunfire exploded behind me. Instinct made me twist my head, which saved my life as the bullet whizzed past my ear. It burnt my skin as I dropped to the ground. That's when I saw Ursula a few feet from me. I crawled towards her as the ringing in my ears competed with the dust stabbing at my eyes. I reached for her leg when somebody pulled it away from me. Then they kicked me in the stomach.

I rolled back as the smoke dissipated, holding my guts as I glanced up to see the men load Ursula into the rear of the ambulance.

'Should I shoot the other woman?' one said.

The other man shook his head. 'We haven't got time for this. Leave her and get in the front. I'll look after the wraith.'

Wraith. That was the word Gideon had used for time travellers.

But how had they known Ursula would land there now, at this time? Gideon had said one of their agents was suspicious of Ursula because of her purple hair and strange clothing. But that ambulance had arrived far too quickly for anybody to have sent a message to the Static about her.

So they must have known she would land there. And only a time traveller could have told them that. So was it a Watcher or one of the Queens of Heaven who was helping the Static?

Or somebody else?

And why?

As the ambulance drove away, all those questions pounded in my brain, but I memorised the registration plate. They could dump that or change the vehicle once out of sight, so I needed to react. I was close enough to see inside the vehicle as two goons clambered into the rear with Ursula, and two in the front, including the driver.

I'd take them by surprise and transport into the back. But I couldn't do it now. A jump close to this would leave me in agony and no use to Ursula or me. So I'd have to wait before appearing inside it. Three minutes? Two? Anything less would debilitate me with pain. So it would be better if they didn't drive too fast, and I could run quick enough to keep up, which seemed unlikely.

They slammed the door and started the engine. My spine clicked into shape as I bolted upright, muscles in my legs throbbing, but at least I could stand. My hands shook as my heart trembled like a kid on a first date. The ambulance moved forward. If it vanished out of sight, I wouldn't be able to hop into it. Travelling into moving objects was always fraught with danger. If I got it wrong, I could hit the ground behind it or appear in front and get thumped.

I counted the seconds in my head. They went by slowly as the ambulance appeared to travel at supersonic speed. Thirty seconds went by before I sped after it. I was a decent runner, but the fight with the men had only added to the pain the bombing had left on my body. My feet ached as I bounced over the ground, running across the damage from the bombing and thankful the debris slowed the vehicle.

A minute flew by, and I could only see the ambulance's rear. If I didn't do it soon, I'd lose it, and the picture in my mind wouldn't help me, not if it were moving too fast.

I closed my eyes, recreated the vehicle's interior and found the trigger.

I landed with a thump, hitting the side as fire raced across my skin. My organs felt like they were inside a microwave as I jerked my elbow upwards into the bloke nearest me. The pointed end of my bone caught him in the throat. He crashed backwards onto his compatriot leaning over Ursula. The two went tumbling to the bottom of the vehicle in a cacophony of obscenities.

Pain rushed through me, a thousand tiny knives sticking into every cell. I plunged to my knees and saw the weapon somebody had dropped. My vision blurred as I scooped up the pistol and turned, firing blindly but hearing the bullets hitting soft flesh. They cried in agony as I fell forward. The one in the passenger seat twisted to see what was happening, so I smashed him in the face with the gun. Then I pushed the barrel into the driver's cheekbone.

I gritted my teeth as I spoke. 'Where are you taking her?'

'I... I...,' he stammered.

Behind me, the other two groaned. Every inch of me was inside a volcano before it exploded, and it took all my strength to stop from blacking out.

'Keep your hands pressed on the wounds, and you'll be okay.' I kept my eyes on the driver. 'Don't make me repeat the question.'

'They told me to take her to Whitechapel.'

'How fitting.' A sudden flush of adrenalin kept me awake, but my arms ached again, and my legs desperately needed a rest. 'Turn around and go in the opposite direction,' I commanded the driver.

The protest died on his lips as I pulled on the trigger. Then, as he took a sharp corner on the road, I switched my attention to the two bleeding behind me.

'Jump out of the back,' I said.

They hesitated and looked at each other in confusion. If my pain was written all over my face, they might have thought it worthwhile trying to rush me. I had to nip that in the bud before I passed out, so I pointed the pistol at the closest bloke.

'Do it now, or I'll shoot you both.'

He didn't wait, kicking open the doors, leaping out of the moving vehicle and hitting the road. The other one followed, and I watched them roll away as I closed the door. I sat and pushed my back into the metal. The driver was still advancing, but there was no telling how long he'd listen to me. The air shimmered around me, and I didn't know how long I had left before I Collapsed. I had to get rid of him.

I returned the gun to his face. 'Pull over.' He didn't waver, hitting the brakes hard, so we jolted forward. I pointed at the passenger I'd clocked in the head. 'Push him out.' The driver did as instructed, and I climbed into the vacant seat. 'Time for you to get out.'

He slipped out of the ambulance, and I joined him. The streets were empty, everybody having found shelter from the raid. I tried not to think about what was happening in the Underground. My legs trembled, and I didn't know how long I could stay awake.

'I'm only a driver,' he said through quivering lips.

'Do you have a good memory?' He was confused for a second before nodding. Fear of death had swallowed his tongue. 'When you return to your masters, tell them a man called Gideon will betray them in the future.'

My words flummoxed him as I whacked him on the side of the head. He hit the ground in a heap. It was painful, but I managed a grin as I vanished, memorising the street sign.

I reappeared and fell at Dash's feet.

'Ruby,' she shouted as she grabbed me.

'Good to see your cat reflexes are up to scratch.'

'Are you okay?'

'You need to go to Fernlea Road, fifteen minutes after my last hop. You'll find me there in an ambulance,' I said before disappearing.

I hoped I'd got the time right, or I'd be in even more pain when I reappeared. I landed next to Ursula, desperate to stay awake. It didn't take long for the stars to twinkle into nothingness as a blanket of darkness swept over me.

Chapter 2

The Stones of Time

The darkness engulfed me for an eternity until it split apart, and I was lying on that pier again in 1882. The sea mist caressed my cheeks, and the air smelt of fire. The faceless people hovered over me. Were they my parents? They made no move to help as the wood stabbed my back. Nobody else was there, not even Diana.

Then voices drifted over me, children laughing and talking. The pain in my legs and chest stopped me from getting up, but I craned my neck to look at the kids, startled to see two versions of Daisy running around me: one with half of her face burnt away, the other peering at me through dead eyes and pale flesh. They spoke to me in unison.

'You couldn't save us, Ruby, so how can you save yourself?'

Electricity shot through me as I lifted my arm, reaching for them and failing. Instead, they clasped hands and danced together, singing a song I recognised.

> *Ring-a-ring o' roses,*
> *A pocket full of posies,*
> *A-tishoo! A-tishoo!*
> *We all fall down.*

They laughed as they sang, gazing at me through those deathly faces. The sweat poured over my head and clung to my hair. When I touched it, great white strands came away from my fingers and dropped into a ground of squirming worms trying to climb up my legs. The smell of burning wood and brimstone filled my nostrils and slithered into my lungs. I coughed so hard I thought I might choke.

I breathed with great difficulty as the girls skipped around me and sang at the top of their voices. This continued for a minute before they stopped and loomed over me on either side. Above them, the sky darkened, and the passing gulls transformed into giant vultures. Then the girls spoke as one.

'The whole world is falling down, Ruby, and it's all your fault. Nothing can change it now, no matter what you do.'

They offered their hands to me, and I took them, feeling cold flesh as they dragged me up. When I stood, they vanished, replaced by visions of Diana and Gloriana. The two women looked at each other and shrugged before turning back to me.

'I saved you, but you abandoned me,' Diana said.

I put a hand on my chest and tried to speak, but only worms cascaded out when I opened my mouth.

'The Queens of Heaven are coming for you,' Gloriana said. 'But even they can't repair the damage you've caused to time.'

They shimmered in front of me as the vultures swooped and shrieked above my head. Then the birds dove straight at me. They struck together and shoved me over. I hit the ground, which wasn't grass or concrete, but thousands of those worms crawling everywhere. A vulture sunk its teeth into my shoulder, and I screamed. Then, with my mouth wide open, the worms crawled inside, their shiny, slimy skin sticking to my tongue and throat. My hand trembled as I reached for my face, only to find my fingers missing and inside the vulture's jaw.

I screamed silently.

Then the darkness reappeared for a second before being replaced by a bright light and somebody shaking me. When my vision returned to normal, I saw Dash driving the ambulance. I gazed at my quivering hands and touched my face, thankful to find it worm free. A herd of bees buzzed inside my skull as we sped forward, the city nowhere in sight.

'How long have I been out?'

'About four hours,' Dash replied. 'The road system in this period is diabolical, but we should be there soon.'

There was a crick in my neck as I twisted my head to watch the English countryside pass us by. Moonlight shimmered over the land, casting a silver glow over everything. The full moon hung low in the sky, hovering over the fields of wildflowers that stretched out as far as the eye could see, bathed in a ghostly light. The petals of the flowers seemed to glow from within. The sight banished my thoughts of vultures and worms, though I felt the inside of my mouth to be sure.

'We're going to the base?' I stared at Ursula sleeping in the back.

'I can't think of anywhere else to take her. Can you?'

I couldn't. And it was why we'd had the base built five thousand years ago, so we had a refuge throughout history.

Stonehenge appeared through the front window, a mist surrounding it as I moved forward. My skin felt like I'd sat in a microwave for the last four hours while steel weights replaced my blood and bones. My head vibrated on another frequency, giving me the worst hangover ever.

Dash pulled up close to the stones. 'We'll get her inside. Then I'll dump the ambulance and see you downstairs.'

The sky was dark. Only a shard of moonlight illuminated the heavens. The sleep had refreshed my body and spirit even though I still ached everywhere. Ursula was motionless as a block of ice. I would have thought she was dead if I hadn't noticed her chest moving a tiny fraction.

Dash slipped out of the ambulance. 'I'll get the passageway open.'

I peered at the stone circle for the thousandth time in my short, long life. When I commissioned the builders of Frixion Prime to construct an underground dwelling, I intended to hibernate there until I was sure the Watchers had stopped looking for me. Once I rescued Dash, it became our official living space whenever we were on Earth, regardless of which period we were in. It was good to have somewhere to hide from the outside world and relax. The Frixions built an excellent security system and were renowned throughout the universe for keeping their client's work to themselves: apart from the fact they always left behind a single item at the site which only they – and the client – could identify as their handiwork. In our case, it was the henge monument they left topside. I wondered what their ancestors would think about the stones erected around it over the following centuries.

Dash opened the back door, and I climbed out. The mist hovered everywhere, sending a chill through my skin. I heard birds crying somewhere above me and imagined those vultures returning. Then I whispered those words the two Daisies had sung.

> *Ring-a-ring o' roses,*
> *A pocket full of posies,*
> *A-tishoo! A-tishoo!*
> *We all fall down.*

'What?' Dash said.

I flexed my arms and ignored her question. 'Help me get Ursula out.'

Dash went inside and lifted Ursula's head while I grabbed her feet. As gently as we could, we removed her from the back. Then we stood the unconscious Watcher up and placed her arms over our shoulders.

Dash peered at the stones. 'We haven't been here before in this time, have we?'

'Don't worry, Dash; we're safe.'

My perfect memory told me we'd never visited the base in 1940, so there was no danger of walking inside to see other versions of ourselves. I felt bad enough as it was without having to deal with that.

We took an arm each and dragged Ursula over to the door, my fingers brushing the thin leather gloves she wore. We entered the lift to carry us below and away from potentially prying eyes. The Frixions had thrown in a foolproof chameleon security system so nobody could see the lift or what was below ground, regardless of how sophisticated their scanning equipment might be.

'I made sure the heating was on,' Dash said as we sank below the stones.

'How was Daisy?'

Since hopping into the oncoming Blitz, the kid's face had never escaped my mind. Ursula's slow, laboured breath rested on my neck as we reached the bottom. The door opened, and the familiar aroma of cherry rainbow drops wafted into my senses; another little Frixion touch.

'When I left, she was devouring all the chocolate ice cream and watching some crazed cartoons on the big screen TV. I told her I'd be back in a few minutes.' Dash's words came out in a rush. 'I don't think we should leave her alone for too long.'

'Are you worried about her?' I said as memories of the two Daisies from my nightmare repeated that nursery rhyme inside my brain.

Dash shook her head. 'I'm more concerned about what she might do to this place without supervision. She is curious, unaware of the potential dangers around her.'

We carried Ursula into the medical room built thousands of years ago. All the equipment and medicines were from hundreds of years in the future. As we laid her on the bed, I had the terrible feeling nothing we had would get her out of the coma.

'I'll check on Daisy while you dump the ambulance. Ursula should be safe for a bit on her own.' I was missing the kid, and it surprised me. 'We need to keep Ursula fed and watered while she's like this, and then we can figure out how to wake her up.'

Dash nodded before disappearing. I sat at the end of the bed, ensuring Ursula was as comfortable as possible. How hard did that pole crack her on the head? I got a damp cloth and cleaned the dried blood from her wound. Her pulse and breathing were slow, but stable. I touched her purple hair and wondered how close a friend she'd been to Diana. Was she a Watcher who'd experimented on me? I rolled up a sleeve and gazed at the symbols on my wrists, watching as they appeared to move in front of my eyes. I knew it was an illusion, but it was still a curious sight. Had the Watchers branded me like an animal? Was that all I'd been to them, and now they, or their splinter group, the Queens of Heaven, would track me down like an escaped stray?

I touched Ursula's cheek and listened to her breathing. After what Gideon had said about her being in a coma for seventy-plus years, I had no fear she'd get worse in the five minutes I'd be away. But how would we remove her from the coma?

I left her and returned to our other unexpected guest, vanishing in one time and reappearing in the same spot decades in the future.

I grinned at Daisy and her chocolate-covered face. 'How are you doing, kid?'

'Do you have more ice cream?'

She wiped her arm across her mouth before licking her fingers clean. Two empty tubs lay dumped on the floor. I strode towards her and grabbed her hand.

'I'll get you some later.'

I took her into the same room where we'd laid Ursula eight decades ago. It was empty. Was Ursula gone because we'd saved her or because we hadn't?

'I'm hungry.' The kid's appetite was endless.

'I need to clean your face.' I spoke to Daisy while peering at the space where Ursula had been. I grabbed a cloth from the sink, wet the material and dabbed at the kid's chin. She squirmed, twisting her cheeks and lips into an uncomfortable-looking expression. 'There, you're brand new now.'

Daisy scampered into the main room, giggling as only a child could. I remembered how she'd looked when we'd first met – at the end of the pier years from now – one half of her face burnt beyond recognition. Then we changed that, and Daisy's father killed a newer version of her: two tries and two mistakes. Two Daisies. And in the back of my mind, they continued to sing that nursery rhyme to me.

'I smell like a lemon,' Daisy shouted.

'What are we going to do with you, kid?'

The question was more to me than her. We couldn't keep her with us – our lives were too dangerous for that – but I was unwilling to dump her with social services. Yet what choice did I have but to abandon her? As I'd always believed my parents did to me.

I threw the cloth into the sink and stared at the empty bed again. The kid shrieked with pleasure in the other room, signalling Dash's return.

'Do you know where I put my communicator?' I asked Dash, watching her grab the kid and swing her around. The longer we kept Daisy with us, the harder it would be to give her up. Already my heart was experiencing sensations both terrifying and exciting.

'You left it in your room before heading for London,

remember?' She spoke through a mouthful of Daisy's fingers. I nodded in reply. 'I warned you not to take it.'

She didn't want me leaving future tech in the past, not again.

I strolled to my room, seeing the communicator on the bed. Once, it had been an ordinary twenty-first-century mobile phone until I took it and one other to the technocrat planet of Yuma and had the devices augmented to perform functions way beyond their original design.

'I want you to come with me and look at Ursula,' I said to Dash as she spun Daisy around the place. I wanted to say something about not having room for a cat to swing a kid, but was too perturbed by her furrowed brow.

Dash widened her eyes and glanced at the girl. 'You don't need me to check Ursula's medical condition.'

I guessed she didn't want to leave Daisy alone again. 'You're the doctor in our partnership.'

I searched for the biological scanner on my updated phone. Dash dropped Daisy to the floor, the kid's face transforming into a colour signifying she might return some of that ice cream from where it came. Daisy fell into a chair, grabbed hold of her stomach, and let out a mighty groan.

Dash stared at her new friend. 'My medical knowledge hardly covers human biology.'

'Quite,' I said as I found what I wanted. 'But I'd like you to come with me. Daisy will be fine on her own for a few minutes, won't you, kid?'

The girl rubbed her gut and whimpered. I grabbed hold of Dash's arm and pulled her toward me. Daisy stopped groaning, flew from the chair, and ran into the kitchen.

'I'm still hungry!' she shouted. Dash shook her head and pursed her lips.

'Stick her in the bathroom with a bucket and some Alka-Seltzer. She'll be fine.'

Dash didn't seem convinced. 'No.'

I craned my neck to see what Daisy was doing. 'You can come right back, one second after you left, and throw up with her. It'll be a true bonding moment for you both.'

Dash shook her head. 'You'll not make the mother of the year like this.'

'I hope not. I'm far too young to have kids.'

She glanced at Daisy as the kid rummaged through the kitchen for more food.

'As long as we're not gone for too long, Ruby.'

'No more than five minutes.'

I smiled at Dash while she grimaced before we both disappeared. We landed five minutes after leaving Ursula. She was in the same place as before, her purple hair shimmering in the light. I took the communicator and ran the scanner across her body, concentrating on the bump on the skull.

'What are we going to do about Daisy?' Dash said as I handed her the device once it had completed its job. I was too preoccupied to give the kid's future much thought, so I blurted out the first thing which entered my head.

'We could reunite her with her mother.'

I was pleased with my ingenuity. Dash flinched at the idea, those wild eyebrows standing to attention.

'Rescue her from death?' She was too surprised to assess the information on the screen.

'Isn't that what we do all the time? Saving innocents from a fate they don't deserve?'

She peered at me. 'I must admit, Ruby, I've been uneasy with our actions lately; acting like gods, saving lives, rewriting history.' She turned away, staring at the data I'd given her.

'Is this your faith returning to you?'

'I'm not sure.' She focused on the screen. 'There are worrying shadows here on Ursula's brain, which I don't think were caused by the blow to her skull.'

She pointed to the images, high-quality pictures of the inside of our patient's head. I peered at them but didn't know what I saw.

'What are they?'

'These dark parts on her frontal lobe aren't normal, plus the regions around the Hippocampus are smaller than they should be. So I think she may have had a pre-existing condition that added to the blow, and is preventing her from waking up.'

'What can we do about it?'

'We can't do anything.' Dash handed the device back. 'We don't have the expertise or the understanding to release Ursula from her prison.'

I sat down with a heavy heart, her words confirming what I'd already thought.

'Then we need to bring the expertise to us.'

'Bring a doctor here from some point in humanity's future? How would we do that? We can't transport other living things through space or time using the Rings.'

I had an idea, but Dash wouldn't like it. 'Which planet has the foremost medical knowledge in the universe?'

She patted her paws together. 'That would be Kaladan.' She sounded surprised. 'You intend to travel to Kaladan and get them to teach you how to revive her?'

I got up, pressed my fingers into my hands, and smiled at her.

'I wish I could, but Kaladan is one of the many planets

with a warrant for my arrest.' I handed her the phone. 'You're the trained physician, the one with an aptitude for this thing, and with me being a criminal there....'

Dash shook her head and looked confused. 'You stole from them a thousand years in the future, or should that be, you will steal from them?'

I put my arm around her shoulder and gave her my most understanding expression.

'It was their future and my past, but it doesn't matter. You're the best of us for this, the most qualified. So I'll stay here and take care of Daisy. It will be good practice for me, just like you said.'

I ushered her into the kitchen and thought about the kid in this same spot years from now. Dash had a misty look in those big feline eyes, and I assumed she knew we had no other choice if we wanted to revive Ursula. And without Ursula, we had no chance of finding Diana.

'Let's go back and talk to her,' Dash said.

I nodded as we time-hopped together.

Chapter 3

Ruby's Diary

Day One Hundred and Eighty-Two, Year One

Earth Time: Unknown. Location: The Library.

Nico was blasting out of the speakers as Diana walked into the library. I put down da Vinci's *The Codex of Leicester* and stared at her grimace.

'Do you need to have this racket so loud?' she said.

'You're not a fan of the Velvets, then?'

She waved her hand in the air, and the volume decreased. 'How can you concentrate when it's so noisy?'

It was rare to see her so grumpy. 'Bad mission?'

Diana threw her data communicator next to the computer and removed her jacket.

'I got the short straw, spending two days in a Berlin bunker in April 1945.'

The thought of it made me grimace. 'Did you learn anything?'

'Only that you can't bring reason to the unreasonable.' She peered at my latest book. 'How have you been while I was away?'

'I searched for them again.'

'Searched for what?' she said.

I peered down the vast length of the library. 'The doors. A way out of here.'

Diana pointed at the Time Ring on the shelf behind me. 'You can leave any time you want, Ruby.'

I glanced at the device. 'Maybe. I'd still like to see how to get in and out of here the conventional way.' I got out of the chair. 'And it would be nice to know where and when this place is. What if something goes wrong when you're away, and you don't return, and the Ring quits on me? I don't know where we are, never mind at which time. Are we on Earth or another planet?'

'Okay,' Diana said. 'Follow me.'

So I did, marching past the computers and books as Nico sang about being a mirror. We reached a blank wall at the end, and she placed her hand on it. It slid apart to reveal a gap into another room. Diana stepped inside and flicked a light on. I followed, surprised to see a home cinema studio.

'Have you been making movies?' I said.

She laughed. 'Not here. This is to watch your favourites on a big screen instead of hurting your eyes gazing at a computer during your regular movie marathons. So now you can look upon Louise Brooks, Humphrey Bogart, Mae

West, Chaplin, and all your other favourites, as they were intended to be seen.'

I ran my hands over the soft velvet of the seats. 'That's great, but it doesn't answer my question.'

Diana walked to the side of the screen and repeated the trick with the wall and her hand. I followed her through the door and into a small gym.

'You need to keep fit as well. The missions in time and space will get more arduous, and you must learn how to defend yourself. Starting now.'

She strode to a mat in the middle of the room and kicked off her shoes. I raised my eyebrows at her.

'You want to fight me?'

Diana lifted her hand and beckoned me to her. 'Unless you think you're not up to it?'

I laughed as I went. 'Good job I'm wearing a t-shirt and shorts.' I flexed my fingers. 'Are there any rules to this scrap?'

She grabbed my neck and threw me to the floor, which I hit with my shoulder. Pain shot through me like a lightning bolt, rushing down my arm and jumping into the rest of me.

'No rules,' Diana said. 'Just like if you get ambushed on a mission.'

I stood, my arm aching, as I twisted my neck from side to side. 'I should warn you, Diana, I've watched every Bruce Lee movie at least twice.'

She rubbed her hands. 'Who do you think taught him everything he knew?'

I shook my head, knowing she was messing with me. Then I attacked, launching a series of swift kicks and punches, but she dodged them by stepping out of the way. I landed on my feet with the adrenalin shooting into my chest. My breath came in quick bursts as heat inflamed my face.

'You were right, Diana, this is fun.'

She grinned. 'We haven't even started, Ruby.'

I circled her, watching her all the time. 'What do I get if I win?'

'What you asked for. I'll show you the way out of here.'

'So if I don't win, you'll keep me in the dark?'

She didn't move as I kept on circling her. 'How's that for motivation?'

I lunged at her, throwing a punch she blocked with her arm. My fist struck a bone, and it was like hitting a brick wall.

'Shit!' I shook my hand and hopped on one leg. It was all she needed, and she kicked my standing leg in the knee, so I collapsed. She could have pinned me to the ground but didn't, moving back and grinning at me.

'Are you sure it wasn't Bruce Forsyth videos you watched?'

She pressed her finger into the wall, and the music from the library filtered into the gym. Nico was wondering what the poor girl should wear to a party as I considered my options. Diana was bigger and more experienced than me, but I had something she didn't: desire. So I pushed off the ground and flew at her like a flying rat, my arms outstretched, ready to dig my nails into her neck. She went to block me again and succeeded, but I swung my foot out as she did this time. I caught her hard in the stomach, and we fell together. I landed on top of her, smirking like a drunken fool.

'Oh, wasn't that a shame, Diana?'

She beamed at me. 'You don't get anything for a pair in this game, Ruby.'

'What?'

Her hands were on my belly, and she dug her nails into my gut.

'Fuuuuu...!'

Diana threw me into the wall as I swore. I hit it and crashed to the floor as she got up and dusted herself down.

'You're hot-headed, overconfident, and take too many risks.' She loomed over me. 'What would happen if somebody caught you during a mission and forced you to tell them where this place is?'

I rubbed the spit from my lips. 'Who would do that? Do we have enemies?'

She turned her back on me and went to the door. 'I'll set the invisible doors to recognise your DNA, all apart from the exit. You're not ready for that yet.'

My body trembled as I stood. 'Who is after the Watchers, Diana? Who should I be worrying about?'

Chapter 4

The Doors of Perception

As we returned, Daisy sprinted into the room carrying a sandwich concoction of her making, smelling of peanut butter, mustard, half a banana, and a slice of cheese. She let out a huge burp. We gave her our sternest looks, so she giggled, dumped the food on the table, and scampered to the toilet.

Dash turned her nose up at the grub. 'I thought you enjoyed taking risks; why don't you go to Kaladan?'

I considered it as Daisy groaned a few feet away. Then I

took Dash's arm and pulled her towards me. 'I'd love to, but you're more qualified than me.'

'And what if I can't find what we need to revive Ursula?'

'Then we'll think of something else; we always do.'

Daisy ran out of the toilet and pushed past us. The smell made me pinch my nose.

'Don't go in there,' she shouted before throwing herself in front of the TV. Dash sighed and put one paw over her face.

I laughed at my friend. 'Or you can stay here and clean the bog.'

She grimaced, glancing between the kid and me. 'Okay, I'll do it. Give me fifteen minutes.'

She disappeared as a rancid puff of smoke drifted into the room. Then it was my turn to sigh and find the cleaning utensils. So I tended to my chores and contemplated the problem of our current guest and not the one eight decades in the past. The kid had shown no adverse emotions with us regarding her new situation. She hadn't mentioned what happened in her house nor spoken of her father apart from that brief conversation with me. She'd never questioned how it was possible to jump through time and space, nor wondered how a walking, talking cat could look after her. The kid was in denial, and it seemed up to me to talk her out of it. She was sitting in front of the TV, munching her dreadful sandwich while watching a cartoon featuring a talking cow. I sat beside her, holding my nose away from the smell of her food. I pointed at the screen.

'What's this about?'

She ate as she spoke. 'That's the Bullfather, and he controls all the talking animals who want to kill the humans and rule the world.'

'So, it's a comedy?'

Daisy turned to me with mustard-stained lips and a glint in both eyes.

'No, you see, nobody understands that animals can talk. So a teenage girl tries to help and stop the humans from hurting them while another teenage girl is an assassin tracking down the formula that lets people understand what the animals are saying. And the two girls are enemies. There's nothing funny about it.'

I decided to cut to the chase. 'Who do you want to live with, Daisy?' Subtlety was never something I was good at.

'I'll live with Dash,' she said without hesitation.

'You will?'

'Yeah. She can be my Mom now.' She didn't look at me. 'Where do you live?'

Daisy focused on the TV, watching as two talking cats fought to the death. I picked up the remote and switched it off. She huffed and turned to me with a scowl, with bits of cheese sticking to her chin.

'What do you think happened at your house, with those strange people?'

'My dad is a criminal.' She didn't speak like a kid, with experience burning behind those eyes that should never have been in anyone so young. She had a childhood she wanted to forget, while I had one I couldn't remember. 'Those men must've been some of his friends. Then Dash rescued me from them.'

The seriousness of her voice worried me. Had she witnessed the violence in that house? 'Did you see what Dash did?'

Her eyes lit up like the sun. 'Sure. She told me to hide in the cupboard, but I watched her through a crack in the

34

door. They were thugs, only there to hurt you. I heard their leader say that.'

She was talking about Gideon. 'Did any of them harm you?'

Daisy shook her head. 'Nah, I was too clever for them.'

'How?'

She grinned at me. 'I told them the police were coming to lock up my dad. They were all worried then, apart from the leader.'

'Do you miss your father?'

Her face darkened in an instant. 'No. He was always horrible to me. I don't want to see him ever again.'

I sighed in relief, knowing I'd got one thing right in framing Dale Lynx for a bank robbery so he could never hurt his daughter again. But that still didn't solve the problem of what to do with her. And it didn't answer why she'd taken to our new world so casually.

'What do you think Dash is?'

The reply was as quick as a flash. 'She's my friend.'

'Yes, but you know she's not like us. She's from another planet.' Was I breaking this kid's heart?

'Of course, she is; I'm not stupid. And you travel through time.'

'How do you know that, Daisy?'

She jumped off the sofa and went to the pile of science fiction pulp magazines stacked in the corner. She grabbed the top one and showed it to me, with the cover featuring people in space suits firing ray guns at a giant alien creature destroying a base on a moon.

'I've read about spaceships and time travel and watched loads of TV shows and movies. I know who *Dr Who* is. So I knew it was all real, even though my mom never believed me.'

I was glad she said that. It made the next bit easier. 'Yes, you're right, time travel is real, and that's how we got you away from those men who wanted to hurt you.'

She dropped the magazine back into the pile. 'Why did they want to hurt me? Was it to do with my dad?'

'Sort of,' I said. I didn't have the heart to tell her it was all a trap laid by Gideon and the Static to catch me. And I had something more important to say to her. 'So, because time travel is real, I can save your mother, and you will be with her again.'

'My mum is dead.' Her voice never wavered, eyes fixed on mine. 'You can't bring her back. You're not God.'

She was right, I wasn't, but I could reunite Daisy with her mother. All I had to do was travel back and remove her from the situation where the car killed her. But how do you explain that to a kid? Even one who believed in time travel.

'Who's your favourite *Dr Who*?' I said.

She beamed at me. 'Well, I like them all, even the ancient ones in black and white. They're funny, with their cardboard monsters and things always falling apart.' She narrowed her eyes as if in deep concentration. 'But my favourite Dr is always the next one.'

'What do you mean?'

'If you think about it, and not just for *Dr Who* or TV shows, or anything, but if you focus on the next thing instead of worrying about the past or what's happening now, then you'll always have something to look forward to, don't you think?'

I gazed at her and knew this was how she was dealing with the turmoil in her life. She appeared to be able to shut it all out and concentrate on what came next, regardless of what had gone before. At least, that's what she was showing us. But, of course, she could just as easily be storing up a lot of problems for further down the line.

Before I could reply to her intriguing question, Dash returned.

'There's good and bad news,' she said as Daisy grabbed her around the waist and buried her face in Dash's stylish velvet jacket.

'Give me the good news first.'

Dash stroked Daisy's hair while she spoke. 'The exalted medical experts of Kaladan told me it is possible to revive our patient from her coma; we only need to ease the pressure on those unusual parts of her brain.'

Daisy lifted her head and stared at me. Did she understand what we were talking about, or was she waiting for an explanation of how I could save her mother?

I smiled at her. 'Would you like lemonade?'

She eyed me with suspicion before nodding.

Dash gave me a puzzled frown. 'Did something happen while I was away?'

I waved my hand at her. 'No, of course not. We were just getting to know each other.' I continued to smile at the kid. 'Follow me then, Daisy. I keep the good stuff hidden so Dash can't steal it.' I turned my back on her and strode into my room, heading for the fridge and two glasses. A pair of young feet stomped behind me as I poured the drinks.

'Mum always used to give me cake with lemonade.'

The fierceness had left her eyes, replaced with a sadness I was all too familiar with.

'Sit on the bed with me, Daisy.'

She did, and I handed her the fizzy pop. She scooped it out of my hand and swung a large gulp into her mouth.

'This is nice,' she said.

I sipped my drink as Dash joined us.

'What's the bad news?' I said.

Dash pulled in her chest and reached inside her jacket to remove a small black box.

'Ursula's treatment can't be administered from outside her body; we need to use these.'

She handed me the container as I finished my refreshment. Daisy rested her head on my shoulder, and I watched her eyebrows flicker.

I opened the container and stared at the two tiny circular objects. 'What are these?'

'The Kaladanians told me the glitches on Ursula's brain are manifestations of some psychosis she's experiencing. So the only way to remove the problem is to enter her mind and talk her out of it.'

Dash looked at me as if she was describing a routine medical procedure: maybe it was on Kaladan.

'And how do we do that?'

'The devices in the box are a transmitter and receiver. One is injected into the subject, while the other is taken by whoever performs the technique. They form a mental link allowing the patient and doctor to communicate with each other within the patient's unconscious state.'

'It sounds groovy. We better get back there so you can do it now, Doctor Dash.'

She grimaced and shook her head. 'I can't do it, Ruby; it has to be somebody with the same biology.' She let that information sink in as Daisy snored on my shoulder. I moved to one side, and the kid slipped onto the bed. Dash was bemused. 'Did you drug her?'

I made sure Daisy was comfortable. 'It was only a small sedative. She'll be out for an hour while you watch over me as I creep around inside Ursula's head.'

Dash gave me a cat grunt as she pushed me away, sitting

next to Daisy and staring into her eyes. She checked the kid's pulse and heartbeat before scowling at me.

'Damn it, Ruby. You can't keep doing this to her.'

'At least you know she won't get into trouble while we're away. Then we need to sort her out with her mother when we return.'

I stood and prepared to hop back to 1940. Dash glared and growled at me in unison.

'You can't give a ten-year-old a powerful drug.' Dash spat a few hairs at me. 'Again.'

'That kid's a strong one, believe me. Now, are you coming with me or staying here to sulk?'

I held the box and disappeared into the past, arriving next to Ursula ten minutes after I'd left. She slept as smoothly as Daisy did in the future. I placed the devices in the palm of my hand. They felt warm and alive, as if they wanted to jump out of my skin and run away. It was a curious sensation. Dash appeared in front of me.

She continued to glower. 'I'm not happy with you.'

'How much did these cost us?'

The Kaladanians were notorious for driving a hard bargain. Dash removed a syringe from her pocket.

'They didn't cost us anything.' She snatched one of the tiny devices from me. 'We owe them a favour. They'll contact me when they want to collect it.'

She inserted the device into the syringe, moved to Ursula, and placed it near the sleeping woman's neck. I didn't enjoy having to owe the Kaladanians anything: they were the Mafia of interplanetary space travel.

'Do I have to swallow this simultaneously as you inject the other one?'

'That's what they told me.'

'And then what?'

New technology always fascinated me, but I had visions of standing under a shrinking ray and swimming through Ursula's bloodstream. But, unfortunately, to my knowledge, no such thing as a shrinking ray existed in the known universe.

'The two devices will connect automatically, and you should find yourself inside her thoughts. Then you talk to her.'

Dash's apparent belief in this increased my confidence a tad.

'Okay.' I slipped the device into my mouth.

'Be careful while you're in there.'

'Why?' I mouthed without moving my tongue.

'Anything that happens to you in there will affect your body here.'

'Great,' I replied as I swallowed, sitting on the bed and peering at Ursula's feet. Sudden panic seeped into my veins. 'How do I get back out?'

Chapter 5

The Long Goodbye

I rubbed at my face as the stars fell over my eyes, and everything vanished. A black cloud settled over me like a thick, impenetrable blanket. Complete darkness engulfed me, and I couldn't say or hear anything. There were no sensations in my body, no feeling of my chest moving up and down, no motion in my arms or legs. I'd slept inside a sensory deprivation tank for an hour once, and this was worse than that.

Maybe I was in a coma.

That was positive; at least I could still think. If I was in

Ursula's thoughts, I might need to use my thoughts to find her. The words came without me moving my mouth.

Where are you, Ursula? Bring me to you.

I waited. There was no sense of time in the darkness. I might have been waiting there for an eternity, but glittering, flickering lights appeared high above my head and a few yards away. I saw my arms and feet as my heart pounded, my chest ready to break and split open. My stomach lurched as the smell of burning rubber smashed into me and infected my head. I took a deep breath as the lights moved from above to in front of me, leading me on.

I walked towards the illumination that grew larger and brighter. I ran, an unknown urgency speeding through me. There were noises at the other end, the movement of human bodies and somebody speaking. My legs stirred beyond my control; Ursula's mind must have pulled me to her. I reached out with mine, searching for her as bright sunshine caressed my face. I looked up and marvelled at the twin moons shining above me. They seemed familiar, but nothing came when I tried to access the memories of the planets I'd visited. Usually, it was as easy as accessing the menu on an old DVD or a computer system, where I flicked down a list of text or images. But it was missing when I reached for that point in my mind. And it was the same for the trigger to the Time Ring. Yet, I didn't worry and assumed it was due to this bizarre process of entering Ursula's mind. Perhaps I couldn't access my memories while I was inside hers. Still, I knew who I was and why I was there.

And since I was experiencing one of her memories, I decided to explore it.

The ground was a deep red, and strange, spiky plants dotted the terrain leading to a lake. I went to it, seeing it full of a vibrant purple liquid. Several peculiar creatures drank from it. One had multiple eyes and elongated limbs, while another had a long, serpentine body and a set of glistening wings. They jerked their heads up as I moved closer and stared at me. That's when I wondered if I could feel pain in this memory that wasn't mine. Dash had warned me that whatever happened here would happen outside, so I guess it could, and I needed to be careful.

'Don't worry, Ursula; they won't hurt you.'

I turned to the sound of the voice, seeing a middle-aged woman that must have been Ursula's mother since they looked so similar, apart from the lack of purple hair. Near her was a child, probably six years old, that had to be Ursula. She held a bouquet of colourful flowers whose scent reminded me of strawberries.

'You shouldn't be here,' she said.

I thought it was to me until I realised a man was behind me. He approached the mother and daughter.

'Why aren't you returning my calls, Cassandra?'

Cassandra went to the man and dragged him from her daughter. Ursula ignored them and moved to the edge of the lake. And I went with her, drawn there by unseen fingers. The strange animals peered at us before proceeding to drink from the water further along.

The lake was a beautiful, transparent purple, surrounded by lush green trees and wildflowers. The sun shone, casting sparkling light on the water's surface. The scent of strawberries filled the air as exotic orange birds sang over the lake. Schools of exotic blue and orange fish swam just beneath the surface, with scales that glimmered in the sunlight. They created ripples as they darted through the water.

Ursula dipped her fingers in the lake as she stared at me. 'You shouldn't be here.'

I smiled at the six-year-old version of her. 'Are they your parents, Ursula?'

She glared at the man. 'That's Duke Particcio, the man who murdered my father.'

I glanced at the dark-haired man as he grasped for Cassandra's hands, and she pulled away.

'Is this an important memory for you, Ursula?'

She tore petals from the flowers and threw them into the lake. 'All memories are important, Ruby.'

'You know who I am?'

Ursula spoke over the raised voices of the adults. 'You've invaded my mind, Ruby, so I know who you are. And you shouldn't be here. Just like him.'

As she studied me, I noticed a large fish swimming in the deeper part of the lake. It was a majestic golden specimen with a long tail and fins that seemed to sparkle in the sun. It swam in slow circles as if it were the lake king.

'I need to get you out of here, Ursula.'

She pointed at the golden fish. 'That's not native to this water. It was introduced two years ago against the protests of locals and those who monitored the ecological equilibrium in this environment.' It was strange to hear a child talk like that until I remembered she wasn't a child anymore, and I realised my being there was infecting her memory of this event. 'What do you think happened then?'

I gazed at the golden beauty, seeing its wide eyes staring back at me. 'It ate everything else in the lake.'

Ursula laughed. 'That's right, which was exactly what the locals and ecologists told the man who introduced it into the water. Can you guess who that man was?'

I nodded at Duke Particcio. 'Why did he kill your

father?'

She threw the last petals into the lake and aimed for the golden fish. It dodged them easily and swam closer to the edge as if taunting her. Ursula clutched the decapitated flowers and turned to me.

'My life gets worse at this point, as soon as my new step-father gets my mother and me behind closed doors. Then, just when I think things can't get any worse, they do. As you're about to discover.'

The lake and everything else disappeared in a swirl of dust. It spun around me in a torrent and threatened to snatch me and throw me out of her brain. But, instead, it vanished as quickly as it came, and I was in a different place. A smell of burning flesh crawled over me and forced its way into my head. I put a hand over my mouth and staggered forward before letting go and throwing up all over a sickly green-looking liquid. I coughed and lowered my head, realising that was where the toxic fumes were coming from.

I wiped vomit from my mouth, stepped back and gazed across the landscape. Then I gasped. The sight before me was the lake from before, with the shimmering waters, vibrant flowers and the golden king of the water now gone.

'Isn't it terrible how certain people can kill the most beautiful things for profit?'

This Ursula was older, a teenager, her expression showing the life of somebody three or four times her age.

'What happened?' I said.

She had more dead flowers in her hand. 'Social inequality, social disorder, corruption, incompetence, pollution, environmental disasters. Add those and others to greed and a ravenous desire for power, and this is the result.' She threw the shrivelled blossoms into the toxic lake. 'Don't worry, Ruby; only one more trip for you.'

The dust reappeared, a whirlwind that surrounded me like a glove. This time, I covered my face until the phenomena vanished. Then, I removed my hand and watched as dozens of men laboured to cover the devastation with fresh concrete.

'What is this?' I said.

An older Ursula appeared at my side, now looking close to my biological age.

'My world is on its last legs, Ruby. What you see are sticking plasters administered by desperate men, but the most desperate explore more creative avenues to keep themselves in power.'

Before I could ask her what she meant, I saw five figures striding towards us. They wore long robes, their faces covered, but I knew who they were: Watchers.

'Why are they here, Ursula?'

She had no flowers this time. 'Duke Particcio sold me to them. He said they've scoured the universe for a girl like me but didn't explain what that meant.'

My throat gasped for water. 'Can't your mother stop him?'

Her sigh carried the weight of the world in it. 'My mother died five years ago. I'm his to do with as he pleases now.'

The Watchers inched forward, but I still couldn't see their faces. Was Diana one of them? Gloriana?

'You can fight them, Ursula, these Watchers. I'll help you.'

She shook her head. 'You don't understand, Ruby; these are the Queens of Heaven. There's no hope for me, but you should flee. Run and keep running. Don't ever look back. Please don't believe anything any of them tell you. It's all lies.'

The Queens reached Ursula and surrounded her until they submerged her beneath their cloaks.

And then they turned to me.

The light came first. It flashed before my eyes and blinded me. I fell to the side, banging my hip into a table. I surveyed my surroundings and recognised it as a laboratory. It was a vast industrial space filled with gleaming stainless steel surfaces that hummed with the sound of machinery. Rows of glass beakers and test tubes bubbled and steamed on long countertops while advanced computer screens displayed data and diagrams on the walls.

I closed my eyes and searched for Ursula in this memory, only to recoil in terror. Ursula was scared, which meant I was.

'Make sure she can't move.'

The female voice was ahead of me and one I didn't recognise.

'I'm ready now.'

This was a different voice, but one I knew: Diana.

I stopped moving. There was light everywhere, a group of people in front of me.

'Diana,' I shouted.

My initial reaction was to run to her, but she neither saw nor heard me: how could she when it was only Ursula's memory? Instead, two women held Ursula down on an operating table. Diana stood over her while behind her loomed five other women: Watchers. My heart thumped faster than it should have, and my legs trembled as I stumbled towards the table.

'Ursula,' I yelled as I slipped between the prison guards and peered at her.

'You shouldn't be here,' she said. Mania was in her bloodshot eyes, spittle falling over her lips.

'Start the procedure,' the tallest of the Watchers said.

'Yes, Ishtar,' Diana replied.

Ishtar! These were the Queens of Heaven. And Diana was one of them or worked for them. This was something else she'd kept from me. I watched her approach Ursula, the scalpel shining in her hand as she grabbed hold of her friend's wrist. Had she really been her friend if she was involved in whatever these experiments were?

I looked at Ursula's skin, stamped with the same three dark oblong symbols I had on my body. My head ached, kicking myself for not checking her hands when we'd got her unconscious body back to the base below Stonehenge.

Diana cut into the flesh, and Ursula screamed. I shoved my fingers over my ears, incapable of removing my gaze from the blood dripping onto the floor. Ursula shivered on the table, and so did I. A cold stab slithered up my arm and over my shoulders. My brain told me to fall and curl into a ball. But instead, I stared at the woman who'd helped me escape from similar experiments. The marks on my wrists vibrated as she sliced into Ursula.

Ursula howled again, her pain transferring to me, the symbols burning on my wrists and back. I crumbled, and my knees cracked into the floor. But my physical pain was nothing compared to watching Diana torture the woman she claimed was a friend.

Just like I'd been her friend. But she'd helped me escape from the Watchers.

I sat there, helpless, sobbing inside as my heart ached.

When Diana finished cutting, she placed a thin metal slice into the incision. I looked at my hand and recognised what the metal was. It was a Time Ring stretched out as one long piece of material. Diana used a laser to fuse the flesh.

Ishtar loomed over Ursula and peered into her face.

'Now, child, use your mind.'

'You shouldn't be here,' Ursula shrieked, fighting against those who held her. Then, finally, she bolted upright and stared at me.

Ishtar turned from the screaming girl and glared at Diana. 'We need to try the spinal cord instead. And the girls must be younger; eighteen is too old. Start at fourteen on one of our blank slates.'

She dismissed Diana and joined the others as they left the room.

Then everything went dark again.

Between one second or a million years, some time passed before I heard the sobbing. Then, the scene changed, and I was back in London, in the Blitz, just before the pole hit Ursula on the head. She stared at me, only it was the other me, me lying on the ground trying to protect the child from the impending destruction.

'You shouldn't be here,' she said again.

'We both shouldn't be here,' I replied. 'I'm going to take you back with me.'

We were frozen in time two seconds before the accident. She shook her head.

'No, it's too late for me. First, find Diana in the loop. And then stop them before they destroy everything.'

'Stop the Watchers?' I said. She smiled at me, a warm smile that melted my heart. 'No!' I screamed as the debris hit her, and it went black again.

I woke up shivering, tears in my eyes.

Dash helped me up. 'What happened?'

My body shook as I went to Ursula and checked her pulse. 'We need to keep her alive.'

'Of course,' Dash said. 'And then what?'

'Then we find the loop.'

Chapter 6

Ruby's Diary

Day Two Hundred and Seventy-Five, Year One

E arth Time: May 1962. Location: London, UK. (Planet Earth).

I pulled at my clothes as I sat, the first time I'd worn a dress since my parents gave me away. The audience was buzzing with excitement as the three men made their way to the stage to receive their Nobel Prizes in Physiology or Medicine. Watson, a tall, lanky man with unkempt hair, looked slightly overwhelmed as he approached the podium. Crick, with a twinkle in his eye, grinned as he shook hands with the presenter. Wilkins, looking dignified in a well-tailored suit, nodded as he received his prize.

The presenter spoke. 'It is my great honour to present the Nobel Prize in Physiology or Medicine for 1962 to Dr James Watson, Dr Francis Crick, and Dr Maurice Wilkins for their groundbreaking work in determining the structure of DNA.'

The audience applauded as the men took their seats on the stage. Watson looked out at the crowd with awe and disbelief while Crick and Wilkins exchanged a knowing glance, both clearly proud of their achievement.

The presenter continued. 'Their discovery revolutionised our understanding of genetics and laid the foundation for modern molecular biology.'

I watched them receive their awards, my mouth open and pulse racing as I sought the trigger in my head and disappeared. I reappeared in a room in 1958, hearing the slow breathing of the woman in the bed near the window. She moved her head to look at me as I took the seat next to her.

'You're not my doctor.'

'No, I'm not, Rosalind,' I said. 'Are you okay to talk?'

She touched her top lip and coughed. 'Lift me up, and we'll see.'

I helped her, my hands on her arms, and noticed her thinness. Being close to death was a regular occurrence in my second life.

'Would you like anything?' I said.

Her lips shivered as she spoke. 'I didn't think I'd see you again, Ruby.'

I held her hand. 'Yet here I am, Ms Franklin.'

Rosalind found the strength from somewhere to shake

her head. 'Ah, but you also told me you were a time traveller, and I didn't believe that either.'

'I've seen your future, Rosalind.'

Ms Franklin laughed. 'So have I, Ruby, so have I.'

Her fingers were cold in mine. 'You get the credit you deserve, and your work, your photograph, changes the scientific world beyond recognition.'

'It wasn't only me, Ruby. Don't forget my assistant, Raymond Gosling. I couldn't have done it without him.'

'Of course,' I said. 'Of course.'

'It was worth it, then?' Rosalind said. 'What I did.'

I nodded. 'You changed the world.'

'And look where it got me.'

I smiled at her. 'Do you want me to sit with you for a while?'

She squeezed my fingers. 'Yes, Ruby. But tell me, have you already visited the younger me?'

I shook my head. 'No. How old were you?'

'Seven, seventeen, and twenty-seven. What is it with you and the number seven?'

I shrugged. 'Just a fluke, I suppose.'

'Well, come here. I want to explain DNA to you.'

We sat together, her talking about science and me telling stories of the alien worlds I'd visited. Then, when she slept, I pulled the trigger to visit the younger versions of her.

I appeared in the garden in front of a seven-year-old Rosalind Franklin. She didn't seem surprised to see me.

'You're not God,' she said.

Her smile was infectious, and I grinned. 'That's true.'

She stepped closer to me. 'God doesn't exist. If She did, She would have made a better world than this.'

I couldn't argue with that. She grabbed my hand and dragged me away from the house.

'We can't let nanny or my brothers see you, mysterious stranger.' She gazed at my clothes. 'I assume you're a scientist.'

I nodded. 'My name is Ruby.'

She offered me her hand. 'I'm Rosalind.'

I shook her hand. 'I know.'

Rosalind let go of me. 'You're from the future.'

'That's right. I can't tell you anything about it, just to encourage you to continue your studies.'

She peered at me through curious eyes. 'I read Mr Wells's book, and I know you can't change history.' I didn't reply. 'So you're here as an observer or a tourist?'

'Something like that.'

'Can you take me with you to see the great events of history?'

I shook my head. 'Sorry, but it's not possible. But I can tell you what I've seen. Would you like that?'

Rosalind craned her neck to stare at the Moon. 'Tell me about other worlds.'

So I did.

Seventeen-year-old Rosalind was less interested in alien civilisations than seeing what 1937 Britain had to offer a year before she would go to university. It was a chilly evening in London, and the Electric Cinema in Notting Hill was bustling with patrons eager to see Laurence Olivier and Vivien Leigh in *Fire Over England*. It was Rosalind's idea to go to the movies when I reappeared in the garden.

'It will stop my family from asking me who you are.'

As we settled into the plush seats, the lights dimmed, and the projector flickered to life. I watched her face in the illumination from the screen, glad to be doing something that wasn't only collecting data for the Watchers. And Diana had been right – watching a movie on a big screen was far superior to peering at a computer.

Rosalind and I spoke little that night until we left the theatre, and she asked me when I'd see her next.

'I'll surprise you,' I said as I vanished.

The remnants of war still littered the streets of Paris in 1947. Crumbled buildings stood alongside newly constructed ones, a constant reminder of the destruction and loss the city had endured. But within the rebuilding, there was a sense of hope and determination.

Dressed in our finest attire, we walked arm in arm down the Champs-Élysées. Rosalind spoke non-stop, her voice ringing out amidst the bustle of the crowded avenue. We passed sidewalk cafes, their tables overflowing with patrons sipping on *café au lait* and smoking cigarettes. The smell of freshly baked croissants wafted out of the patisseries.

We saw a small art gallery as we turned down a side street. The works of up-and-coming artists filled the windows, many of them survivors of the war. We stopped to admire the pieces, the vibrant colours and the bold brush-strokes.

'Are you enjoying your work in the lab?'

Her eyes lit up like the Parisian sky. 'Oh, yes.' Rosalind grabbed my hand. 'It's so refreshing not to be the only woman in a laboratory and to be treated like a human being, not an interloper.' She gazed at me. 'Do the male time travellers treat you as an equal?'

'I thought you didn't believe me about the time travelling?'

We stopped near the Seine in sight of the Eiffel Tower. 'How else am I to understand you looking the same as you did twenty years ago when I first met you in the garden?'

'Indeed. And I'm grateful you've allowed me to record your life this way.'

She touched my arm. 'Yes, but why me?'

'Why not?' I said.

'There must be thousands of people more important than me.'

'Everybody is important, Rosalind. Now tell me about X-ray diffraction and DNA.'

Chapter 7

Gloriana

Dash's hair bristled as she narrowed her eyes. 'What's the loop?'

'I don't know.'

I told her what happened inside Ursula's head about Diana, the experiment, and the Queens of Heaven but left out what I'd witnessed of Ursula's upbringing. I didn't think it was right to repeat those private moments of her life without permission. It was bad enough I'd invaded her mind in the first place, but I could excuse that as a medical emergency, even though I hadn't helped her wake up.

Dash considered my words, rubbing at the fur on her chin. 'Diana experimented on Ursula?'

I nodded. 'That was in her memories.'

She pointed at my wrist. 'So she might have helped the Watchers experiment on you?'

I shrugged. 'I guess so, but there is another possibility.'

'What?'

I tried not to think about what I'd witnessed inside Ursula's head.

'If the Queens of Heaven are a renegade faction in the Watchers, then the Watchers may be unaware of these experiments.'

'But you did see Diana cut into Ursula while the girl was awake?'

The memory was burnt into my mind forever now. 'Yes.'

Dash turned her paws into fists, and I saw the frustration seeping out of her.

'So she lied about your parents giving you to her in 1882, and she probably helped in the experiments her friends conducted on you? And you still want to search for her? Why?'

'I don't know the truth about any of it, Dash.' I moved to the wall, raising my hand to slam into it but stopped when I heard Daisy snoring behind me. 'I won't know what happened until I speak to Diana again.' My shirt and jacket had slipped down, revealing those marks on my wrist. 'Ursula had these as well. When we return to her in the past, we must check her hands.'

Dash shook her head. 'I understand you wanting to discover the truth about your missing memories, Ruby, but surely you don't trust Diana anymore after this?'

I wasn't sure if I did or not. 'On the pier in Saltburn in

1882, Diana told me the Watchers were holding her prisoner, so maybe they forced her to perform those experiments on Ursula.'

'And on you?'

'Possibly, and maybe that's why she helped me escape from them. I owe her my life.'

'Or she might have taken it from you.'

'Which is why we need to find this loop, whatever it is.'

'And how do we do that?'

The frustration was mine now. 'I don't know, but we have to try.'

Dash returned to the sleeping girl. 'I won't leave Daisy alone again. If the worst happens to us, she'll be stuck here on her own.'

Guilt seeped into my bones as I stared at the kid snoring on my bed. I'd failed to save Ursula from her nightmare; I couldn't do the same with Daisy.

'Can you pick up the medical equipment we require to keep Ursula comfortable in 1940?'

It was tempting to search every nook and cranny of the base to see if I hadn't hidden the comatose woman somewhere. But I didn't.

Dash sat on my bed and made sure the kid was okay. 'Sure. I'll get what we need for now from this period and more advanced medical supplies in the near future. What are you going to do?'

'I'll hop back six months and save Daisy's mother.'

Dash may have had second thoughts about changing history, but her face told me she knew we had to do this. Once Daisy was with her mother, we could focus on finding this mysterious loop.

'Fine, as long as you handle it with care and discretion. I

don't want you blundering in as normal and making things worse for Daisy.'

'Cheers.'

'How will you do it?'

I went to the computer and found the details of when and where Lucy Lynx had died.

'I'll find her, explain everything, and see what she says.'

'You'll tell Daisy's mother you're there to prevent her death?'

'It's the best solution in this situation.' I wasn't sure if I believed that or not.

'How will you reunite the two of them?'

I didn't know. 'I'll think of something.'

Sadness engulfed Dash's eyes as she peered at the sleeping child.

'Okay. Daisy should wake up in the next half an hour. Should I wait for you in this here and now?'

I gazed into her eyes and saw something I hadn't seen before during all our adventures. In our time together, Dash had hidden her sorrow from me about being the last of her people. Not once had I considered she might have wanted to be a mother before her planet had died. And then learning what she'd lost with her nest made me realise how selfish I'd been.

'Of course,' I said. 'Then we can look for Diana.'

I didn't expect that to be easy, having no idea what Ursula meant by the loop. But that wasn't the priority. Instead, I pictured the image and details I needed of the time and location of Lucy Lynx's death. Then I thought about the date and vanished as Dash cradled Daisy in her arms.

I landed in the shadows next to the railway station, my

hand finding a damp wall in an alley. The smell of fresh pizza drifted through the air as I heard a train arriving. I inched towards the road, watching as the carriage rolled to a stop. Then the doors opened, and the passengers stepped out and into the sleepy seaside resort of Saltburn. If I'd got the timing wrong, most of them would have seen me appear, another example of the recklessness Dash wanted me to eradicate.

Many times over the years, I'd appeared in places out of nothing to find people gawping at me as if I was a ghost. In one sense, I suppose I was. Or a wraith, like Gideon and the Static thought of me and the other time travellers. I was a phantom – a phantasm lingering in fake memories, only existing in a time I couldn't remember.

But this time, I was lucky enough to have hopped into an isolated spot, landing unseen and not scaring any locals.

A local: that's what I'd thought I was to this place – born in 1868, leaving in 1882. Yet, I wasn't. So I checked my surroundings, hoping some missing memory would flash back into my brain. It didn't, and I returned my focus to saving Lucy Lynx. Warm sea air drifted across my face as I recalled the details again: an accident was about to happen in this spot. I walked towards the expected point of impact, scanning the area to find it empty. According to contemporary reports, there were no witnesses, and the police never found the driver. But deep in my mind, I expected to see Daisy's father, Dale, driving the car that would kill his estranged wife. Something in the hit-and-run details made me think it wasn't an accident and somebody Lucy knew must have been behind the wheel. And he was the likeliest suspect.

I checked the area, but there was no sign of Daisy's

mother. The train had left the station, and all the passengers had dissipated, leaving me the only one there. But where was Lucy Lynx?

Right on cue, a woman strode out of a side street and looked in my direction. She waved her arms at me and shouted.

'Down here, Ruby.'

It wasn't Lucy Lynx.

It was Gloriana.

Shit!

She gestured for me to follow her as she ducked into a café. There was still no sign of Lucy, thirty seconds away from her recorded death. I waited until it passed her allotted demise, curious about Gloriana's appearance and concerned about my ability to save Daisy's mother. Seagulls flittered around my head as I searched for her or the car, perplexed when neither appeared. Had I got the place or time wrong? Perhaps my trip into Ursula's mind had scrambled my brain. I rechecked my perfect memory and found the same results: Lucy Lynx should have died in that spot. Now.

But she hadn't.

That might have seemed like a good thing, but I didn't know where she was. And if I couldn't find her, I wouldn't be able to reunite her with Daisy unless I went further back in time. I stored that possibility in my head and strode towards the café, entering cautiously and inspecting the place. Apart from the staff, there were four other people. Two older women sat in the corner arguing about the state of the country while Gloriana was at a large table with a woman. Was this another Watcher? The exiled time traveller beckoned me forward with a flick of her fingers. I slid into a seat opposite them, glancing out of the window, expecting to hear the screech of tyres and a scream.

'How nice to see you. I've ordered a pot of green tea for four.' Gloriana smiled at me and turned to the woman sitting beside her. 'Lucy, this is Ruby.'

The chair nearly fell from under me, my legs adjusting to the shock. Daisy's resemblance to her mother was evident, with the same piercing blue eyes and striking platinum blonde hair. But, compared to her daughter's long flowing locks, Lucy's was cropped short, as if some manic hairdresser had taken a pair of blunt sheers to it in the dark. I scrutinised Gloriana to see if she was any different to the person I'd encountered six months in the future, looking for her Time Ring but finding nothing on her fingers. Maybe this was an earlier version of her, and she didn't know we'd already met. The arrival of the fourth guest to our soiree answered that question.

'Gideon, this is Lucy,' Gloriana said as the Static man slipped into the seat next to me. 'Try to be nicer to him this time,' she said while staring at me. He was so close I could have wrung his neck. I concentrated on her instead.

'Where's your Time Ring?'

It had to touch her skin to work; the thought process for travelling through space and time wouldn't work without that connection. As I scanned every inch of her, it crossed my mind how similar it was to the procedure I'd undergone getting into Ursula's mind. Did the same people create both sets of technology? Were my hops through the universe down to the technocrats of Kaladan?

Gloriana poured us all a cup of tea when the pot came.

'Time Rings are such a thing of the past.' She smirked at her little joke. 'What you need is something which gets right under the skin.'

The implication sent a shudder down my spine. 'It's implanted inside you?'

My mind flashed back to the scene in Ursula's mind and the experiment forced upon her. And Diana's involvement in that. Gloriana sipped at her tea and grinned. A hint of lemon sprang from the teacup, combining with Gideon's spiced cologne, forming a heady mixture attacking the front of my skull.

'Are you the one who told lies about me to my predecessors in the forties?'

The scowl on Gideon's face matched the bitterness in his voice, eyes narrowing to the point they might disappear from his head.

'Are you as horrible as the last version I met?' I said to him, not waiting for a reply and returning my gaze to Gloriana. 'I guess Diana completed her experiments.'

I thought about what I'd witnessed inside Ursula's brain, the scalpel slitting open her wrist while she was still awake, her screams and the blood on the floor. A disturbing itch crawled across my neck as my wrists trembled.

'Oh Ruby, you have no idea what Diana has been doing through the centuries; your friend kept so much hidden from you. But don't worry; I'm here to enlighten you.' She broke a biscuit in half and dropped one piece into the cup while chewing on the other. 'Of course, she had to test it on herself first once she let you go.' Small crumbs were glued to her chin, tumbling over the table in a fine mess. 'What a muddle that could have caused.' A manic grin covered her face. My pulse increased, and I regretted not bringing a weapon with me.

'Why did you betray me to the Static at Daisy's house?'

I hadn't forgiven her for that. Lucy flinched at the sound of her daughter's name. I glanced at her and wondered why Gloriana had brought her. At least she was safe from the hit-and-run. Gideon laughed while Gloriana continued to nibble on her treat.

'I was fascinated with the myths of the Greek gods when I was younger,' Gloriana said. 'I wanted to have the power to control my destiny, dreaming of being like Athena or Hera, falling in love with Aphrodite.' She nurtured the cup in two hands, sipped at the warm liquid and smiled at me. 'I couldn't have any of that, of course, but I can move the chess pieces of humanity around to improve the lives of our species. Just like you've done since Diana set you free from the cruel touch of the Watchers.'

Half of my brain screamed at me to get out of there, grab hold of Lucy and leave, while the other part needed to discover what this strange woman knew about me.

'Is this why you've brought Lucy here and him,' I nodded at Gideon brooding next to me, 'so you can move me around in some warped scheme of the Watchers?'

She guffawed and snorted tea onto the table. 'Good God, no: I escaped their clutches, just like you did. Mrs Lynx is here because I know you want to reunite her with her daughter. I've told her all about travelling through space and time, but I don't think she believes me.' Gloriana patted Lucy on the hand. Lucy leant forward to say something but stopped, appearing overwhelmed by the situation. I couldn't blame her. 'Gideon is here to prove a point to you.'

'Why did you leave the Watchers?' I said.

She sighed and took Gideon's biscuit from his untouched cup of tea, smiling at me wistfully.

'I was there from the beginning, an original, you might say.'

'And they got rid of you?'

Annoyance flashed across Gloriana's face. 'Imagine you're Florence Ballard, a founding member of the Supremes, and you see yourself pushed out of the group by people you thought were friends, betrayed by the machinations of those with more devious motives than making the world a better place.'

The cup shook in her fingers, voice querulous with glowing red sparks behind those eyes. She put both hands on her head, pushing that dark hair up and down in a rhythmic motion until she appeared to remember where she was. The two old dears in the corner stopped complaining to each other and stared at our table.

'I've always preferred Diana Ross,' I said.

She ignored what I'd said. 'I had to leave before the Queens killed me. Diana would have done the same if she didn't have her fledglings to protect.'

I snapped my head back at her words. 'You mean...'

'She couldn't escape with you, Ruby. She had to stay behind to ensure the Queens don't destroy all of time and space with their experiments.'

'I thought their experiments would be over once it was possible to have the time device inside the body?'

If what she'd just said was true, then Diana's involvement in the Watcher's experiments was to protect Ursula and me.

There was a stab in my heart from the memory of abandoning Diana, of knowing she sacrificed her safety to free me. And there was the guilt from believing she'd lied and betrayed me.

And what did Gloriana mean by fledglings?

'Piffle, my dear girl, you think that was the only experiment they've conducted in the last thousand years?' She rattled the cup in the saucer, the perfect image of how my brain felt inside my skull.

I turned my wrists upwards. 'You mean the experiments they performed on me?'

'On you and many others; you're one of the lucky few who got away.'

'There were others?'

Cold fingers clambered at my heart. I'd gone there to save Daisy's mother, but I thought about my missing past while I looked at Lucy, picturing the other girls they'd experimented on, and it broke my heart.

'Over the years, Diana slipped a few of her pupils into the timeline. I don't know what happened to them, but she told me she hid some scientific discoveries with those kids to keep them from the Queens.' She let me process that information.

'You'll help me and my people find all these secrets and teach us how to use the science,' Gideon said. His smirk was reminiscent of a giant slug I'd encountered once on some desolate planet on the other side of the universe.

'No, she won't,' Gloriana said. 'That's not why you are here. Be patient; we'll get to you soon.' She chastised and dismissed him in one go.

'Do you know what happened to my parents?'

It was all I thought of now. My concerns for Diana, Daisy and Ursula were pushed into some dark corner of my mind, left to wait while I resolved something which had festered for an eternity. She shook her head and twitched her eyebrows.

'Procurement was not part of my remit; you'll have to see Diana about that. But I will help you locate her.' She clasped her hands together and leaned back in the chair.

'Why?'

'Because the Queens of Heaven are all our enemies – they threaten all of history. If they uncover what's inside Diana's head, we will never be safe again.'

'What's inside Diana's head?' I said.

She shrugged. 'Unknown to me but rumoured to be terrible secrets that would destroy everything.'

I gazed into her eyes and figured she exaggerated for her own ulterior motives.

'How will you help me find her?'

Gideon fidgeted in his seat next to me, his face a perfect picture of frustration and desperation. Lucy found the courage to speak; her expression was a cartographer's dream of confusion and misery.

'Where's Daisy?'

Gloriana sighed. 'I told you; you'll be with her soon. Unless you want me to drop you back in front of that drunk driver or return you to your thug husband?'

Lucy was on the verge of tears as I grabbed her hands. So my concern for her meant I missed the importance of Gloriana's words.

'Daisy's fine, trust me. I'll take you to her once we've finished here.' I returned my attention to the architect of this drama. 'Tell me how to find Diana,' I demanded, wondering if I could get my fingers around her throat before she disappeared. The stupid grin returned to her face.

'I will, but you have to promise to do something for me.'

I should have expected it. I never imagined she acted from the goodness of her heart.

'What?'

'You must promise to destroy them.'

'Destroy who, the Queens of Heaven?'

'Them and the Watchers. Find and destroy them, end

everything they are. Then I'll give you what you crave, Ruby Quartz.'

I'd never believed in the Devil, yet now I had second thoughts.

But would I make a deal with her?

Chapter 8

The Immortals of Time

The hate in her voice made Gideon shudder. I had no qualms about dealing with the people who had stolen my life and experimented on me, but I wanted to know why she was so desperate to see an end to them. It couldn't only have been because they'd cast her out.

'Why?' I said.

'Because if you don't, they'll destroy all of time and space.'

I pushed my spine into the chair and scrutinised her face. Was she trying to manipulate me again? I wouldn't trust her or anything she said if she worked with Gideon and the Static. But I still had to listen to her. She might be the only one who could tell me where Diana was.

'How will they do that?'

'Some experiments are too terrible for this world, and even immortals die, Ruby.'

As with most of what she said, it brought me more confusion than clarity.

'As long as we avoid accidents or murderous intentions, the Time Rings keep us alive forever if we don't remove them.' It was one of the first things Diana had taught me. Gideon was shocked at my words; poor Lucy was dumb-founded, all bulging eyes and nervous ticks. 'And since yours is now inside your bloodstream, I think you'll be fine; same for the others who've had it done to them.'

She shook her head. 'That's what we all thought, that science had conquered death, but we were wrong.' Her voice quivered, tripping over the words.

If she wasn't telling the truth, she was the best actor in the world. 'How is that possible?'

'We believed we were immortal, not realising we continued to age at a reduced rate. At first, it was invisible to notice until Diana discovered what was happening.' Sorrow entered her voice and eyes. 'She is the brightest of us all.'

'But we still get to live for thousands of years, right?' So it didn't seem like a terrible fate.

Gloriana removed a small mirror from her jacket, peering into it as Gideon shuffled restlessly next to me.

'When we met in that bar, even in the gloom, I knew you could see it in my face – the way the lines are creeping over my flesh and eating into every part of me. It's only a matter of time.'

I laughed loud enough to make Lucy flinch. 'Look, I hate seeing my reflection at the best of times, and yes, you may have a few wrinkles, but with the Time Ring inside you, altering your blood and DNA, you'll live for thousands of years. It's the same for the Watchers and the Queens of Heaven. They might not be immortals, but they're close to it, so I don't understand what they're worried about.'

'Ruby, you can't realise what these people have become. They've spent so much time travelling through time and space being treated like gods, and it's warped their minds. They crave to live for millions of years; they demand their youth back; they want to control time and space at every possible point. The Queens of Heaven came into existence because they were sick of only recording history. So they need to interfere, to change, and to meddle. Imagine how catastrophic that will be.'

She stared at me, waiting for a response I wasn't prepared to give about what Dash and I had done since I'd escaped from the Watchers.

'Why should I believe any of this?'

'Because, dear Ruby, Diana wanted to protect you. So she made the Queens a promise, the consequences of which will leave no part of the universe safe from their actions.'

'What promise?'

'She promised to continue her experiments for them as long as they didn't tamper with history.' She grinned at me. 'I wonder what Diana would think of what you've done since she helped you escape, of all the times you've altered history on a whim.'

Those cold fingers inside my chest grew in number until an army of ghostly regrets swam through my bloodstream.

'All I'm doing is saving lives; you can't tell me there's

anything wrong with that.' Nothing and nobody would convince me of that.

'But you've never considered the consequences, have you? So, head down, barge in, and ask questions later.'

'What consequences?'

'I thought you'd never ask.' She grabbed the salt and pepper pots. 'The salt represents Lucy, and the pepper is Gideon.'

She held them up before putting them back on the table with a thump.

'Fascinating,' I said.

'You came here to save Lucy from certain death because you felt sorry for her?'

I looked at Daisy's mother, her face a mixture of expectation and desperation, knowing I had to choose my words not to upset her.

'I'm here to make sure mother and daughter are reunited.'

'So, you'll put this version of Lucy with the version of Daisy you have six months from now?' Her tone made me uneasy as I recognised she was trying to trick me.

'What do you mean by version?' Lucy said with a whimper.

Gloriana looked at her through unsympathetic eyes. 'I've told you, you died. If it weren't for me, you'd be lying in the road, broken and bloodied. In the future Ruby has travelled from, you're dead and have been for six months. Daisy went to the funeral and is alone because Ruby organised it for your useless thug of a husband to end up rotting in a cell.' She nodded at me. 'You did a good job there with the one change I'd agree with.' Then she returned to Lucy. 'But I saved you, and now Ruby will have to put you in a safe place until your timeline catches up with your daughter's.'

Gloriana sounded like a stern Victorian teacher scolding a naughty child.

'It's all true, Lucy,' I said. 'This is how I know Daisy is secure.'

'So, who is looking after her while you're here?'

She appeared to have accepted the truth, concerned about what was happening to her daughter. I didn't even attempt to describe who Dash was.

'Trust me, she's fine.'

'Yes, but she has six months' memories of her mother's death,' Gloriana said as bluntly as possible.

'That's better than her being dead.'

Gloriana shook her head and puffed out her lips.

Gideon joined in the conversation. 'She's not getting it.'

Gloriana grabbed the pepper pot and placed it in front of the Static man.

'This is the Gideon in the room with us now.' She seized an identical pepper pot from the other table and stuck it in front of me. 'And this is the Gideon you encountered at Lucy's house.' She brought the two pepper pots together. 'Will this one here catch up with the other one in six months?'

I didn't reply because I didn't care what happened to any incarnation of the man.

'Yes,' Lucy said with a sudden enthusiasm for the conversation. It was probably because she didn't want to think about meeting her daughter, who would have six months of mourning embedded in her youthful mind.

'Come on, Ruby; don't tell me you haven't considered these things while gallivanting around time interfering with the universe's natural order?'

Gloriana picked one of the Gideon pepper pots, poured some on the table, and then did the same with the other, mixing both sets. I watched the contents combine, unnerved by what she was suggesting.

'The Gideon I meet in the future knew who I was, so even though this meeting comes after that one, this one influences that one,' I said. 'It's a temporal paradox. Diana taught me all about them.'

Lucy appeared perplexed. 'What's a temporal paradox?'

I resurrected Diana's explanation from my memory. 'Temporal paradoxes fall into two broad groups: consistency paradoxes like the grandfather paradox and causal loops.' Lucy looked even more confused. 'Imagine you build a time machine, so you travel back in time, meet your grandfather before he produces any children, and kill him. Thus, you wouldn't have been born, and the time machine wouldn't have been built, creating a paradox. A causal loop is a paradox of time travel that occurs when a future event is the cause of a past event, which in turn is the cause of the future event. Both events exist in spacetime, but their origin cannot be determined.'

As exasperation drifted across Gloriana's face, Gideon placed his hands in his head.

'No, Ruby, this isn't a temporal paradox or causal loop. Gideon only recognised you at Daisy's house because I told him who you were beforehand and showed him photos of you.'

Icy fingers clawed at every sinew in my body. 'So, why did you set me up to get captured?'

'I told you; you're a piece on a chessboard being shuffled around by those with greater knowledge than you.' Gloriana snatched both salt dispensers and slammed them in front of Lucy. 'Your daughter went to your funeral, stared at your immaculate corpse in its coffin, watched you being buried and threw dirt over the lid.' She knocked one of the salt cellars so hard it fell over and rolled off the table. 'So, how will you explain everything to her when she sees you again?'

We were alone in the café, apart from the staff cowering behind the counter. I felt the place should have closed ten minutes ago, but they were too scared to come and shoo us away.

Lucy burst into tears. 'I don't know.'

I glared at Gloriana. 'Was there any need for that?'

'This is for your benefit, Ruby. You must understand that you and your furry cat friend are as dangerous to the universe as the Queens of Heaven and their megalomania. What you're creating will tear everything apart.'

Lucy wiped at her cheeks. 'So Daisy thinks I'm dead?'

Gloriana frowned at her. 'Didn't you listen to anything I've said? She went to your funeral. Your daughter doesn't think you're dead – she knows it.'

Lucy ran out of the café with a face covered in tears, her arm resting on the window as she sobbed outside. I had no idea where I'd put her for six months and keep her safe. I couldn't leave her in the base; we'd made too many visits there recently to make that comfortable.

What was I creating?

I glared at Gloriana. 'Was that necessary?'

She shrugged. 'If you continue telling people something and they're too stupid or arrogant to believe you, what do you do? Especially when that information is vital to save the universe and humanity.'

A chill ran down my spine as I remembered being inside Ursula's head, watching Diana cut into her friend.

'With Diana's help, the Watchers experimented on kids – including me – and discovered how to get the time travel technology into the body.' I glanced at the marks on my wrists, realising that Diana had got me away from the

Watchers before they could slice me open. 'But if they've perfected that technique, what other experiments are they forcing her to do?' And did they involve more children, possibly even younger ones?

Gloriana grabbed pepper bits between her fingers and dribbled them onto the floor.

'I'm not sure, Ruby, but they won't be good, whatever they are. You need to find Diana and stop her.'

'And how do I do that?'

She shrugged and didn't answer. Finally, I'd had enough of her lies and manipulation, getting up to join Lucy outside. At least with her, I'd achieved what I'd come for.

Then Gideon spoke. 'Fragments.'

That word stopped me in my tracks. I remembered his future version saying the same thing when he'd crawled across the floor in his blood.

'Fragments?' I replied.

Gloriana emptied the one remaining pepper pot all over the table.

'When you change time, did you think the previous version vanished into nothing?'

'To be honest, I've never given it much thought.'

'Every time you alter history, you create fragments, leaving behind alternate timelines. So there are at least four parallel realities for Daisy Lynx now: the one where she's with you, one where she's dead, the "original" with half a scarred face and the one where she's in school now, not far from where we sit. When you're finished, who knows how many there will be? So that's four realities occupying different levels of the same space; four realities stacked together where there should only be one.'

'Have you ever played Jenga?' Gideon said. I shook my

head. 'Players take turns removing one block at a time from a tower constructed of fifty-four blocks. Each block removed is placed on top of the tower, creating a progressively taller and more unstable structure. You're doing something similar with your time fragments.' He peered at me as if I was one of history's worst criminals. 'Eventually, the whole thing will collapse.'

Gloriana dropped pepper over the floor. 'And the Queens of Heaven know what you're doing.'

I fought the urge to sneeze. 'I've been waiting for the Watchers to come after me since I escaped; surprised to meet none of them until you turned up.'

Gloriana stood and placed money on the table. Gideon walked ahead, peering through the window in an agitated state. What would I do if the Queens of Heaven appeared here? Maybe I could speak to Ishtar about their experiments on me.

Gloriana threw bits of salt over her shoulder. 'You should ask yourself why they've let you run free and wild for so long.'

I had too many other pressing problems to worry about that. Their mistakes were my successes. 'I don't care what they think or do.'

'Poor Gideon doesn't know what's waiting for him when he meets you again in six months,' Gloriana said. He'd gone outside to stand watch while Lucy chewed on a cigarette.

'How do I find Diana?' I said as she made her way to the exit.

'You'll stick to our pact?'

'To stop the Watchers and the Queens from these universe-destroying experiments you keep going on about? Sure, of course, I will.'

I didn't know how I'd do it, but I was willing to try anything. Or at least tell her I was. She seemed to think we'd made a bargain, but I didn't recall making any promises.

She nodded. 'Didn't Diana mention her experiments while training you?'

Gloriana had her hand on the door. I searched my memory of the two years I'd spent with Diana before the escape when we'd visited some of the universe's most beautiful and strangest planets.

'I wasn't aware of any experiments. She kept that part of her life from me.' So she must have been protecting me.

'You'll remember eventually, Ruby, with that extraordinary mind of yours. Don't knock yourself out.' She draped an arm around my shoulder, and her lips pushed close to my ear. 'You know what you have to do with her?' Gloriana nodded towards the shivering Lucy Lynx standing in the street.

Unfortunately, I did.

Gloriana left and dragged Gideon away as I stared at Lucy. I went and gazed into her tear-filled eyes.

'I'm sorry,' I said.

There was no other choice.

I had to kill Daisy's mother.

Chapter 9

Ruby's Diary

Day Three Hundred and Fifty-Five, Year One

Earth Time: 2132. Location: Korda Trading Post. (Planet Zhu).

I waved my arms in the air to attract the attention of the green-skinned woman with long yellow hair. She grinned through gem-studded lips and ignored me as she dealt with the drunk pawing at her. She pushed his head into the wall and broke his fingers, the crack so loud I heard it over the terrible band playing in the bar.

'What's wrong?' Diana said.

I pointed at my food and the prawn-like creature fidgeting on my plate.

'It's still alive.'

Diana bit into a piece of orange bread that smelt like toffee sauce. 'Yes, so you should eat it while it's fresh.'

I pushed the plate away and studied our surroundings. The place was dimly lit, with neon lights flickering above the long, curved bar. The patrons were a motley crew of aliens and humanoids, all with a seedy, criminal air about them. The air was thick with the stench of cheap liquor and something unpleasant that must have been native to this planet but reminded me of wet fish.

The sound of clinking glasses and raucous laughter filled the room, interspersed with the occasional screech or growl from the exotic patrons. In one corner, a bunch of slimy, tentacled beings huddled together, whispering and scheming. At the bar, a giant, hulking creature pounded back shots of a glowing blue liquid while a group of insectoids chittered excitedly in their language.

A droid bartender with a flickering holographic face sauntered towards us.

'Would you like a drink, ladies?'

'A shot of your strongest alcohol for me,' Diana said. 'And a sarsaparilla for the girl.'

The barkeep floated away as I grimaced. 'Sarsaparilla?'

'It's good for you,' she said.

The alien prawn crawled out of the salad and off the plate. 'Unlike this place.'

A group of reptilian creatures sauntered by, their scales glistening in the neon light. A pair of furry, quadrupedal beings played a game of cards in the corner; their sharp teeth bared in fierce concentration.

'Maybe you can tell me why we're here.'

Bits of orange bread stuck to Diana's lips as she spoke. 'Check out the man at the bar.'

It was hard not to spot the only bloke in the place: over six feet tall, muscular, with piercing blue eyes and a face that looked like it had seen a lifetime of troubles.

'Do you know him?' I said.

The green-skinned woman brought our drinks and stared at my cuisine as it slipped off the table to the floor.

'Don't you want that?' she said.

Before I could reply, a small droid scuttled over, scooped up the errant food, and secreted it inside its body. Then it shot away as the woman shook her head.

Diana answered my question. 'The man at the bar is Axel McGurk, a local farmer down on his luck and desperate for money to support his wife and baby daughter. He's here to talk to the woman sitting in the shadows in the far corner.'

I tasted the sarsaparilla, which had a sweet and earthy flavour with a hint of liquorice and vanilla, and glanced at the woman. Her long hair cascaded down her front, and her eyes seemed to glow in the dim light. She sipped at her drink, her gaze scanning the room as if searching for something or someone.

'Who is she?' I said.

'That's Ektryn,' Diana said. 'A fugitive from justice, hiding out on this planet so she can continue her illegal experiments.'

I shuddered at her words. 'Experiments?'

Diana nodded. 'Yes, Ektryn is the foremost expert in cyborg creation in the universe. But, unfortunately for her subjects, Ektryn's zeal for her speciality forgoes any understanding or empathy for the living parts of her creations.

And that's why she's hiding away at the fag end of the universe.'

'And McGurk is going to volunteer to be one of her guinea pigs?'

'He'll be paid handsomely for it, but being this far from the centre of the universe means he's unaware of her current reputation. When she's finished with him, he won't dare see his family ever again.'

The sweet taste of the drink stuck to the back of my throat.

'What will she do to him?'

Diana got up. 'Come. I'll show you.'

I downed the sarsaparilla and followed her, glancing at McGurk as he made his way into the shadows and Ektryn. A cold wind hit me in the face as I stepped outside. The streets were a hive of activity, with several species moving in and out of the shimmering metallic buildings. We strode through a marketplace, the vendors selling a wide variety of stuff, from brightly coloured fruits and vegetables to intricate jewellery and technology. Diana was in front of me talking into her communicator, so I browsed the stalls, marvelling at the alien goods on display and communicating with the sellers using the universal translator implanted near my throat. I touched my skin but couldn't feel the device, only knowing it was there because I could understand those around me. Diana had inserted it while I was unconscious, and the operation had left no scars.

'Are you ready?' Diana said.

I returned the necklace to the store holder, a grey-skinned man with gills, and looked at Diana.

'Where are we going?'

She showed me her communicator, which displayed the insides of a laboratory.

'That's the place straight ahead of us.'

I turned from the screen and towards the building. 'That's Ektryn's lab?'

'Yes. We need to travel three months into the future from this exact moment and time.' She pointed at the image, indicating the far corner of the lab. 'That spot will do. Okay?'

I nodded, and she disappeared. My heart rate decreased as I glanced at the market stalls, wondering if I'd ever return for that necklace.

Then I vanished.

Diana was waiting for me when I reappeared inside the laboratory.

'Doesn't Ektryn have security?'

'A few droids beyond the electrified outside barrier. She doesn't want any eyes, human or other, to see what goes on in here.'

It was a vast, open space filled with gleaming equipment. The walls were made of a sleek, reflective material that changed colour depending on how you viewed them. In the centre of the room was a massive cylindrical machine that hummed with energy.

'What are we looking for?' I said.

Diana led me to the far side and a large container where a shimmering mist obscured its contents. She placed her fingers on the glass, and the haze dissipated. I put a hand to my throat and gasped at what I saw: The only remaining human parts of Alex McGurk were his head, his right arm and half of his chest. The rest had been replaced by shiny silver metal, including legs that had added three extra feet to his height and an axe on the end of his new left arm.

'Welcome to the future of humanity,' Diana said.

I pressed my chest in a futile effort to control my breathing. A shiver ran down my spine as my throat turned into a desert and the sweet taste of the sarsaparilla seemed ages ago.

'Why?' I said.

'Ektryn lost her daughter to a flesh-eating disease. That was the driving force for convincing her she had to find a way for humans to survive beyond the body. This is the latest in her long line of cyborg experiments.'

I peered into McGurk's face, resisting the urge to ask Diana why we were recording this. Then Alex McGurk's eyes flicked open, and he stared at me. His lips trembled as he spoke.

'Help me.'

My legs shook as I stumbled backwards into a table and knocked several beakers and tubes onto the floor. They crashed into dozens of pieces scattered everywhere.

I grabbed Diana's arm. 'We must do something.'

She pulled away from me. 'Nearly a year of training, and you're still like this?'

My arms ached as I bit my top lip, drawing blood and swallowing it as I glanced at the imprisoned Alex McGurk.

'What happened to his wife and baby daughter?'

Diana checked her data communicator. 'Ektryn paid them a handsome amount. Enough to get off this god-forsaken planet and find a better life elsewhere.'

'Do they know about this?'

'I doubt it.'

'So what were they told?'

'She informed them I died in an explosion. That's why Ektryn gave them so much money.'

I turned to McGurk with his words ringing in my ears. 'Did you know she was going to do this to you?'

He shook his head. 'No, this wasn't what we agreed on.'

'I told you,' Diana said. 'She has no ethics or empathy.'

'But I do have a brilliant mind,' Ektryn said as she entered the lab. Her hand never wavered as she pointed the pistol at me.

'What are you trying to achieve?' I said.

She waved the weapon at me to move me away from McGurk. 'Only the most important scientific discovery in the universe: immortality. All flesh is weak, so I must find something to maintain consciousness beyond the natural lifespan of all living creatures.'

'You've tried transferring memories to a machine?' Diana said.

Ektryn nodded. 'Yes, many times. No matter which material I use for the transfer, the memories never transform into fully functional consciousness. All they become is repeatable data, like a digital clip you can rewind infinitely, but that's it. All the humanity is lost.'

I pointed at what remained of Alex McGurk in his prison. 'Do you call that humanity?'

She peered at me as if I was a bug under a microscope. 'How did you get into this facility?'

Diana smiled at her. 'It's okay, Ektryn. We've got what we needed.' She nodded at me. 'Back home, ten minutes after we left.'

Then she disappeared.

'What?' Ektryn. 'The building is protected against tele-porters.'

I moved towards her, and her hand trembled as she waved the gun at me.

'One day, I'll return for him.'

She squeezed the pistol's trigger as I pulled the one in my mind.

Diana transferred data from her communicator into the computers when I appeared in the library.

'Any problems?' she said.

I leaned over her shoulder and peered at the machine, watching the information on the screen. 'You stole from her.'

She shrugged. 'I copied it. She still has it all.'

'I thought we never interfered with history?'

She turned to me. 'We didn't change anything, did we?'

'Not for her or that poor man.'

Diana got up. 'You must be starving since you couldn't finish your food in the bar.' I shuddered at the memory of the living prawn on my plate. 'Do you fancy a burger with fries?'

My stomach rumbled at hearing her words. I didn't reply as she went to the kitchen, ignoring her and gazing at the computer.

Then, nearly a year after my parents gave me away, the first doubts crawled across my brain.

Chapter 10

Secrets and Lies

'You did what?'
Dash's eyes rattled around in her skull, lips trembling and fur standing to attention. Daisy continued to slumber on my bed like a newborn babe.

'Is there any food left?'

I didn't wait for an answer, strode into the kitchen and searched for sustenance as I grabbed a cold beer from the half-empty fridge. Dash followed me into the room, steam spurting from her head. Before she strangled me, I explained what happened at the café, but not all of it: I didn't mention the fragments. That would only upset her even more. I slumped into a seat and drained most of the bottle.

'What did you do, Ruby?'

'My original plan was to hide Lucy somewhere away from here, keep her out of the reach of Gideon and his gang, but from the conversation we had, it was obvious they weren't interested in her beyond getting to me.' As I spoke, Dash's nose twitched from side to side, looking like it was about to tumble from her face. 'That was until Gloriana reminded me that two versions of Daisy existed at that point.'

I decided not to mention four of them somewhere in the timeline. I'd struggled to come to terms with the concept of time fragments, unsure how to explain it to Dash when I didn't understand it myself. Do temporal manipulations create branches in time, unstable dimensional openings, spatial paradoxes, and time loops? That's what Gloriana and Gideon implied with their pepper pots and four versions of Daisy. I'd broken the Watcher's primary rule – only observe and never change time; smashed it so many times I'd lost count. But it was always to save lives or, with the scarred version of Daisy, to improve them. Yet I'd never thought about what might have happened to that existence I'd altered. Did it still exist somewhere as a fragment? And even if it did, then so what? Why did it bother Gloriana and Gideon so much? He'd said all the fragments lay stacked together, and they'd eventually collapse, but he'd never provided any evidence for that theory.

'I have a twin sister?'

Daisy stumbled into the room and wiped the sleep from her face. She walked over and ate the fish from my plate. I laughed and ran my fingers through her hair. She didn't flinch, staring at me with kind eyes. Maybe she'd warmed to me.

'Sort of, sweetie,' I said, snatching a bite of the food before she devoured it.

'You had to bring time into line.'

The way Dash said it made me sound like a god. But I wasn't. I didn't want to be a Watcher who only observed, but equally, I wouldn't be like the Queens of Heaven, believing myself greater than anyone or anything else in the universe.

'Do you believe what we've told you about travelling through space and time?' I asked Daisy.

She nodded as she ate. 'Of course I do. I'm not stupid.'

There was a hint of defiance in her eyes, and I wondered what adverse effects her upbringing might have had upon her. Living with Dale Lynx wouldn't have been easy. Not to mention what the death of her mother had done to her.

She finished her grub and ran around with her hands in the air. I was glad to see somebody enjoying themselves for once.

'I couldn't take Lucy to Daisy in school because that wasn't our Daisy. So I had to kill Lucy off.'

I'd ensured that Daisy was in the other room when I mentioned her mother.

Dash narrowed her eyes at me. 'You faked Lucy's death?'

I sat at the computer and returned the news reports to the screen.

'I thought about recreating the hit and run, but that would have meant cracking a few bones. So instead, I placed her not far from the café and made an anonymous call to the police. There were no witnesses, and the medics said it was a heart attack. So it was easy to fake with the drugs we have that leave the body resembling a state of death. Getting Lucy past the autopsy and dealing with the mechanics of the funeral parlour proved trickier, but it's amazing what you can achieve when you grease the right palms. I even went to the funeral to make sure nothing went wrong.'

Dash didn't appear too impressed by my ingenuity. 'You closed the loop?'

'I had to.' I glanced at the doorway to ensure Daisy couldn't hear me. 'Lucy died again, but differently. So the original events ran forward as before, with Daisy living with her father until we framed him for robbery and brought her with us.'

Dash moved to the door and peered into the other room, where the kid had gone quiet. Then she looked at me.

'She's reading one of your books about quantum physics.'

I laughed. 'She's a clever girl.'

Dash agreed. 'I'm glad you sorted it, but what about the other problem?'

'What would that be?' I'd focused on one difficulty at a time.

'What about Gideon and the Static? Why would a renegade Watcher work with a group of men who want to steal the secret of travelling through space and time?'

'I'm not sure.' Gloriana's motivations were still a mystery.

Dash's fur bristled. 'I don't trust her.'

'I agree. She only revealed those things to force a response from me.'

'She wants you to find Diana.'

'I always intended to find Diana; I owe her that, at least. Now I need to figure out her cryptic clues.'

Daisy ran in and grabbed my fingers. 'I remember you.' Sadness filled her face. 'You were in the corner eating sandwiches while my father got drunk.'

I'd attended the funeral to ensure Lucy didn't wake up and scare everybody. And to watch the murderous parent. Daisy gripped my hand, and I considered what to say to her, settling for something mundane.

'It was a nice spread.'

The mention of food resurrected Daisy's hunger as her stomach rumbled. She let go of me and rushed into the kitchen. It was curious how her memories had caught up with her at that precise point, remembering my presence at the funeral only after I mentioned it to Dash. Beyond saving lives, I'd never considered what my actions did to history and the timeline but had I been more malicious than benign? Had I split time so much it was in danger of tearing apart? Did I believe what Gloriana and Gideon claimed about these fragments?

I gazed at the kid as she rifled through the kitchen.

'Do you have any cakes?' she shouted.

'I have a secret stash of chocolate in the study, Daisy.'

Dash scrunched her eyes and scowled at me. I assumed it was because I encouraged the girl to eat too much sugar. Or maybe she thought I was going to drug her again.

'We haven't used that room in ages,' Dash said.

I raised my eyebrows and beamed at her as the girl scampered toward me.

'Where's the study, Ruby?'

She jumped up and down like a restless jack-in-a-box. The kid had grown fond of me, and I'd taken a shine to her, which I didn't think was possible.

'Come.' I took hold of one hand while Dash held the other. 'We'll take you there.'

I didn't know whose smile made me the happiest: Dash's or Daisy's. I caught my reflection in the mirror and didn't flinch for once. It was a surprise, not recognising the delight on my face. Maybe this was what it was like to be part of a happy family.

We headed down the corridor and towards the farthest end of the base. It didn't matter about Gloriana and her machinations, Gideon and his band of unmerry men, or Watchers and Queens of Heaven. Even the despair of my missing parents and memories disappeared as I enjoyed a child's delight. I opened the door to the study and watched her sprint inside, smiling at the shock on her face as she discovered something far more precious than all the chocolate in the universe.

'Mum!' she screamed as she jumped into Lucy's arms with such force I thought she'd knock the poor woman over. Lucy had gone through a lot in the last six months, starting with the drugs injected into her to slow down her system to the point of death. And me making sure she wasn't embalmed at the funeral parlour. Then there was the pain her body had endured upon resurrection from that state. The drug did the job, but the after-effects could be uncomfortable. Added to that was what had happened to her daughter and the isolation I'd forced on Lucy. I'd made her promise to stay in the study until now, never able to leave, even when she heard Daisy on the other side of the door.

None of that could have been easy.

Dash stared at me. 'I can't believe you did this.'

'I took the risk of bringing Lucy to the base once I decided there was a greater danger of leaving her in a world which witnessed her burial.'

'I'm flabbergasted she never once left the room while she was there.'

'There's a bathroom, a fridge, and plenty of food, so she didn't have to worry about that. There was internet and TV· access as long as she used headphones, so Daisy didn't hear anything. And I told her if she came out before I returned, she'd throw time out of sync again, which would have dire consequences for Daisy and all of us.'

In reality, I didn't understand what would happen if she'd walked out to see earlier versions of us before I met with Gloriana in the café and put this plan together. Would it have created a branch in time, an unstable dimensional opening, a spatial paradox, or a time loop?

Dash gazed at the reunion of mother and child. 'This is amazing.'

'Let's leave them, and we can discuss our next step.'

There were tears in Dash's eyes, for what she witnessed and for herself. She'd developed a bond with the kid, which wouldn't be the same now Lucy was back. I closed the door behind us, and she grabbed my hand.

'I had my doubts about this, Ruby, but I'm so thankful you did it.' She pulled me closer and hugged me. Then, after thirty seconds, she let go. 'You did a good thing here.'

'You're not worried about me changing the past?'

She shook her head. 'Not this time.'

Dash seemed happier than I'd seen her in a long while, allowing me to broach a difficult subject.

'Did you think about having a family on your home planet?' It wasn't very subtle.

She snatched her hand from mine and stormed into the main room. I rebuked myself for asking such a question while wondering how I could make it up to her. Instead, I strode after her as she poured a large glass of whisky. Before giving her my disapproving look, she scuttled in front of a computer and searched for the latest news.

Dash avoided my gaze. 'What will happen to Daisy and her mother now?'

'We can set them up anywhere in the world with new identities. We'll give the kid a life she could never have had before.'

Gideon's words floated around inside my head.

Fragments.

I remembered the first time we'd met Daisy on the end of that pier, with half her face scarred beyond belief. That was the kid I'd wanted to save; it was that Daisy I travelled through time for on more than one occasion to give her a better life. But what if I'd altered nothing, like Gideon and Gloriana claimed, and had only created a newer version of the kid? What if there was still a Daisy somewhere in the universe with that burnt face and monstrous father? What if there was a point in time when my interference had gotten her killed? And if I'd caused fragments in time with her, what about the other times I'd changed history? Why had the Watchers and the Queens of Heaven not stopped me if I'd triggered so much chaos?

Raucous laughter rushed out of the study, a mother and daughter finding each other again. We sat and listened to it, smiling at each other in silence before Dash spoke.

'I'm sorry.' She pushed the booze into the shadow of the computer screen.

'No, it's me who should apologise. I shouldn't have asked you such a personal question.'

She changed the subject. 'I got all the best equipment and medicine for Ursula.'

'I should go back and try again.' Ursula had never disappeared from my thoughts since leaving her in 1940. 'I must have done something wrong last time.'

Dash brought up Ursula's medical scans on the screen. 'I think these dark spots and changes to her brain could indicate schizophrenia.' She pointed to the marks. 'You couldn't ease those, no matter what you did. The doctors on Kaladan must have been wrong with their diagnosis.' It didn't seem likely, more to do with my clumsy stumbling inside her thoughts. 'Do you believe the experiments forced upon her by the Watchers could have caused her illness?'

Anything was possible where my kidnappers were concerned. More worrying was the implication that whatever they did to me could have long-term repercussions. Perhaps I had no memories of my first fourteen years because their experiments had damaged my brain.

Should I get Dash to scan my head? If they'd broken my mind, would I want to know?

'Gloriana told me to search through my time with Diana to recall the experiments she did, which would help me find her.'

I remembered Gloriana's words in the café, hearing her voice. The marks on my wrists appeared to vibrate as I clutched at them. There were two years of memories to assess, all stacked together in my unique filing system, and it would take some time to go through them.

'Whatever experiments she worked on, she must have been successful with some of them.' Dash touched the Ring on her paw. 'To attach this inside the body and get it to work is impressive.'

She was right. 'I'm guessing they managed to link the technology to a person's DNA.'

Dash nodded. 'Like you did with mine and the Time Ring you gave me?'

'Yes, but this must be different somehow, or what was the point of inserting the technology inside the body?'

A flash of memory slipped between my lips as I thought of that.

'Don't knock yourself out.' The words came back to me, but they weren't Diana's.

'What?' Dash said.

'That's what Gloriana said to me as she left the café.' The smirk on her face continued to linger in my mind. 'Ursula was knocked out in the Blitz. Gloriana must know about Ursula and what happened to her.'

That was her hint to me: *don't knock yourself out.*

'Wouldn't Gideon have told her about Ursula?'

'How could he? I changed history to take her from the Blitz and the Static. Gideon doesn't know who she is.'

Dash peered at me as if I was losing my mind. All the talk of fragments was splitting my brain into conflicting parts.

'Her words can only have been a hint about Ursula and the coma she's in. I shouldn't knock myself out because Diana's friend already has. I have to enter her mind again.' I didn't consider if the device in my head was a one-time thing. 'There must be something I missed.'

'It's too dangerous, Ruby.' Concern seeped out of her eyes. 'We don't know why Ursula travelled to that location in the past.'

'She's a Watcher, Dash; that's what they do. Ursula was there to observe a significant event in history, that's all. What happened to her was an accident.'

'But you said the Static arrived too quickly as if they knew she'd be there. How do you explain that?'

'I can't, but it doesn't matter. I have to get back into her mind. Did the Kaladanians say if the communicators were permanent attachments?'

'That was the impression they gave me.'

'I don't see how we locate Diana without doing this.'

It was true, having searched my brain a thousand times since seeing Diana again, trying to identify another solution. Dash huffed and puffed, but didn't talk me out of it.

'Okay, Ruby. We can leave Daisy and her mother for twenty minutes while we do this, but we require a better plan this time.'

She strode over to the desk and handed me the laser weapon.

'Did we have a plan last time?' I laughed as I took the gun from her. 'How am I supposed to take this with me, and why would I need it?'

'Put it into your pocket just in case. Maybe the communicator won't only manifest Ursula's memories when you're inside her head.'

She spoke with such certainty that I questioned whether she'd told me everything the device could do before swallowing it.

'What aren't you telling me, Dash?' I cradled the cold metal in my hand. 'I know you said it could be dangerous, but not enough for this.'

'The communication you have with Ursula is two ways, meaning....'

'She can see my thoughts?'

'It's possible. But as long as you stay in control, I don't see why that would happen.'

'I need to access the memories she has of Diana.'

Previously, I'd gone in intending to haul her from the coma. But I'd lost myself in her past and that horrific experiment memory. The realisation someone had performed those same experiments on me distracted me. And the pain had thrown me – Ursula's suffering as they'd cut into her had transferred to me and scrambled my brain. I couldn't let that happen again.

'Yes, you need to focus on that. How did you end up in that memory last time?'

'I called out to her with my mind and asked Ursula to bring me to her.'

'Then you'll do the same again.'

She was right. It would be simple.

'Let's go.'

Chapter 11

Church of the Poison Mind

I disappeared in an instant. Dash joined me ten seconds later, the two of us staring at the snoozing body of Ursula. I tried not to see myself as an invader preparing to spy on her private thoughts. Dash grabbed my wrist, exposing the physical marks the Watchers had left on me.

No, not marks – they'd branded me like cattle. I was one of their things to play with, to experiment on. I was the property of the Watchers, but it was the Queens of Heaven – a militant splinter of the Watchers – who I'd seen the last time I was in Ursula's mind. They'd experimented on her and others – and me? – and Diana had led those experiments.

'Are you sure you want to do this, Ruby?'

Was I? I wriggled from her grasp. 'There's no other choice, Dash. Gloriana hinted there was something in Ursula's memories to show where the Queens are holding Diana prisoner. So I have to explore her mind to find the answer.'

'Okay. When you get in there, concentrate on Diana and getting Ursula to take you to those memories. Don't go poking into her childhood or thinking of those experiments.'

I peered at Ursula's flickering lids, picturing what was causing so much rapid eye movement. I wanted to touch that flamboyant purple hair, lean over and kiss those lips back into the waking world. But this wasn't a fairy tale.

'How old do you think she looks?'

'I'd say she's about twenty.'

It seemed about right for her physical appearance. I scrutinised her cheekbones and skin, watching her flesh move as the breath crawled from her lungs.

'When I went into her mind and saw her on that operating table, I think she was eighteen.'

Make the next one younger.

Is that what Ishtar had instructed Diana to do? Had I been the next one? Were we sisters, this sleeping woman and I, if not in blood but circumstance? Were we both Diana's friends who she'd betrayed or saved?

'Search for those memories she has after the experiments, of the time she spent with Diana before getting her Time Ring.'

'Perhaps her trip to the Blitz was Ursula's first hop through time.'

If it had been her initial journey into the past, what a

cruel accident for her to succumb to the damage caused by the bombing.

Dash stared at me. 'When you observed that memory of Diana cutting Ursula open, are you sure the experiment didn't work, and she didn't have a Time Ring placed inside her?'

I pointed at Ursula's hand. 'There's your answer. There would be no need for her to wear the Ring if one was attached to her spine.'

Dash shook her head. 'I still don't understand why the Queens are doing this. What's the difference between having the Ring on your finger or inside you?'

I didn't know. 'Maybe I'll find out in Ursula's memories.'

And there were other questions I needed answers to. Had Diana helped Ursula escape as she did with me and those secret others Gloriana hinted at? How many were there, and were they all teenagers like me? Or were they even younger?

The thought of the Queen's experimenting on kids of Daisy's age made my skin crawl, but I assumed it must have happened. And there had to be a way of finding them in time and space. But I had to rescue Diana first, and the only way to do that was to return to Ursula's mind.

'Do you know what to do?'

I nodded and closed my eyes. I only had to find the link again, that connection between us. It wasn't too dissimilar to moving through time and space, just seeking the proper association. I sat at the end of the bed and rested my hand on her leg.

Ursula, can you hear me?

The thought echoed in my head.

Please take me to Diana.

I pictured the two of them together, inside Diana's library, where she'd taught me so many things; and kept so much from me. The image slipped from my mind as an invisible connection dragged my other self like a magnet towards her. Then something threw me into where I'd spent two years of my life. My chin hit the ground, and my eyes flicked open. The room smelt of baked apples, and my jaw ached. I rubbed at it, remembering when Diana would bake or cook for me.

'You might be stuck here with me, Ruby, but at least you'll eat well,' she'd said.

I smiled as I touched my face. There'd be a nice bruise on my chin when I returned to the real world. The library was empty, and bookshelves filled the room. I smelt the dusty aroma of the covers and heard the tap dripping in the corner. Diana had spent two years trying to fix that leak, but she could never get it right. I'd asked her why she didn't bring somebody in to repair it, but she only shook her head.

'This place is only for you and me, Ruby.'

But if that was true, how could Ursula remember it?

Unless?

Had Diana trained Ursula before me? Was I just one of several kids from an assembly line?

I added those questions to all the others and went to the books. I touched the wrinkled, yellowing pages of the closest, reading the title aloud.

'*The End of Eternity*.'

'You'll enjoy that one.'

That was Diana's voice inside my head while I was in Ursula's.

The computers were at the other end of the room, but the collection of books had always fascinated me more. I'd laughed at her at first, making jokes about older people hanging on to their material objects when she could have them all stored electronically.

'Artefacts are necessary,' she said to me. 'Things we hold in our hands and can touch are more important than digital constructs on a screen. The Watchers don't just observe history; they preserve objects from being lost, including all the books here.'

I grabbed *The End of Eternity*, and it crumbled into dust in my hand. As I stared at it, the middle of the room glowed and changed: it was still the library, but now Ursula was strapped to a table as Ishtar towered over her. Ishtar was beautiful, with high cheekbones and full lips, her eyes a deep blue, shimmering like a Caribbean ocean under the sun. She lowered her head and ran her fingers through Ursula's purple hair.

'I thought you'd be the one,' Ishtar said. 'But you let me down.' Then she turned and gazed right at me. 'I guess it's your turn now.'

My heart froze as she moved forward and a fire blazed in her eyes. I wanted to move but couldn't, my legs as petrified as the rest of me. Ishtar reached for my face, and I closed my eyes.

But the touch never came.

Ishtar and Ursula had gone when I opened my eyes, and I was alone in the phantom library.

'I'm sorry for what happened.'

It was Diana's voice from behind me. When I turned, she held Ursula's shoulders, the two of them shaking, vibrating inside their clothes until they stopped and stared in my direction. Bits of the book clung to my fingers as I watched them.

'It's the disorder in my brain which does that,' Ursula said. Diana stood frozen in her thought, but Ursula moved towards me. 'I'm sorry about before, with the screaming; that memory is particularly traumatic.'

'Did the Watchers experiment on you?' I said.

'In a way. The Queens of Heaven forced my friend to cut me open. Do you know who they are?'

I nodded. 'They're a faction inside the Watchers, dedicated to interfering in history to suit their own ends.'

'Never forget that, Ruby.'

Ursula's lips tilted upwards, the dimples in her chin wrinkling closer together, her perfect teeth gleaming at me as she smiled. The sheen on her hair glowed as she reached for me and held out her hand. I took it and felt the warmth at odds with the cold, sleeping woman beyond this realm.

'Are we inside a different memory?'

'This is a sanctuary from...' she struggled for the rest of the sentence. 'Time and space, I suppose.'

'I came here to bring you back to the waking world.'

She let go of me and walked towards the row of computers at the library's rear. Ursula touched the nearest monitor.

'The first time you did, but not now.'

'I still want to get you out of here.'

She flicked through several images on the screen, going too fast for me to see what they were. 'What if I don't want to leave?'

The question surprised me, but I thought about what she'd said about this being her sanctuary. 'You got yourself injured on purpose?'

It was possible. If she'd studied history as much as I had with Diana, she could have known when and how the misfortune would happen during the Blitz.

She laughed and put both hands to her head. 'Don't be silly, Ruby. That was just a happy accident.' Something in her eyes made me doubt her words. 'I can see why Diana likes you so much.'

She returned to the computer and moved through the images quicker than the human eye could process.

'Was Diana your friend?' I said.

Ursula stopped touching the screen, and it froze on a picture of a young girl standing on the beach clutching a bunch of balloons shaped like the planets of Earth's solar system.

'Diana is still my friend, Ruby, as she is yours. Never forget that, no matter what anybody tells you.' She touched the side of her head. 'All the memories you have of the two of you together will never leave you, and you should cherish them for the rest of your eternal life.'

'Do you have hyperactive hyperthymesia as well?'

'A perfect memory? It's close to that.' Ursula smiled at me. 'But there are some things still missing from my mind.' She glanced at the remains of the book on the floor. 'It stops me from getting bored while I'm here. You can only delve into your memories so often, especially when most are distressing.'

'Why don't you want me to help you out of your coma?'

'I'm safe in here, Ruby. But you aren't.'

'What?' The word stumbled out of my mouth.

There was an arm on my shoulder before I could say anything else, fingers pulling me back and flinging me into a tower of books. *The Complete Adventures of Sherlock Holmes* collapsed onto my head, dust blowing up my nose and forcing a hefty cough from my lungs. My attacker obscured my vision, the crunch of footsteps heading towards me. I pushed my nails into the floor, popping my shoulders up and tossing the books away to see who it was.

Could the Queens of Heaven get to me inside Ursula's mind?

'You shouldn't be here.'

I froze when I saw her – not a Queen of Heaven but the manic version of Ursula from my previous visit: the one they'd experimented on. She grabbed my leg and dragged me across the floor. My torso scattered discarded novels and encyclopaedias to form a path for my subdued body.

'I wish I could help,' the other Ursula said. 'But it's getting harder to control the different versions of me.' She rubbed at her temple. 'It might be something to do with that knock on the head I got in the Blitz.'

The manic Ursula tossed me against the far wall like a child throwing its toys from a pram. My back cracked against the plaster, tendrils of agony reaching into my muscles and squeezing them until I could take no more.

'Can't you get it to leave?' I shouted, crawling along the ground to avoid the hands stretching out for me. But it was no good as she put her foot onto my leg so I couldn't move. Next, she pushed her knee into my back as her fingers grasped my neck and dug her nails into my skin.

'You shouldn't be here.'

She clutched at my throat, and I squirmed for breath. My hand slithered inside my jacket, finding the laser weapon, gripping it with my last strength, and thrusting it into her gut.

I pulled the trigger, but nothing happened.

Of course it didn't. Dash had only been half right. It was here, but it couldn't work.

The thought barely made it from my brain as she strangled me. I waited for my life to flash before me, wondering through the pain if, at last, my missing memories would return. The gun clattered to the ground as I dropped it, my hands flailing to get her off my back but only finding empty air. As darkness descended over me, the pressure dissipated from my neck, phlegm chucking its way out of my mouth as I coughed my guts over the floor. I rolled onto my side as lights flickered above my head, my sight returning to see one Ursula whispering to the other. At first, I couldn't tell which was which until noticing the anger in the eyes of the closest.

Then my attacker scowled at me before stomping into invisibility.

'We have little time,' the calm Ursula said as she lifted me. 'I can't keep her away for long. Ask me what you want and then be on your way.'

I coughed again and touched my throat. It was still warm where those fingers had dug into my skin. There would be quite a bruise if I got out of this mess. As I peered at her, something moved in the shadows behind Ursula. My ribs ached from the pressure of my heart pressed against them, expecting more angry versions of her to attack me. But when I looked harder, I saw the younger Ursulas from my previous visit. All three of them smiled and waved at me.

'Do you know what experiments Diana did?'

'Only the last one; she was very secretive.'

She pointed to the computer she was looking at before the other version attacked me. I limped forwards, an ache in my ankle that hadn't been there before being dumped against the wall. Her younger versions whispered to each other behind me as I scanned the documents on the screen. I held my breath as I read them.

'This can't be possible.'

Ursula peered over my shoulder, her face close to mine. I smelt strawberries on her skin and remembered that beautiful, exotic lake.

'It's impressive.'

'I know she's brilliant, but this is....'

'There's a lot more than that, hidden somewhere.'

I took a deep breath. 'What do you mean?'

Ursula's eyelids flickered as if somebody had stuck her head into an electricity socket. I turned my hands into fists in expectation of the other Ursula returning.

'Diana was the cleverest of the Watchers; that's why they had her training all the new recruits.' She smiled at me. 'People like you and me. But her mind could never keep still, so she was always conducting some experiments or research. She loved that as much as working with her kids, but once she discovered the existence of the Queens and what they wanted to do, Diana knew it would be catastrophic if they learned of her results.'

'Was she performing experiments capable of destroying space and time?'

The stare she gave me was the only answer I needed. 'You should leave now. There are other versions of me coming. And they don't like you.'

My hands were behind my back to hide their trembling. 'I have one more question.'

'Go ahead.'

'Can you see into my mind and access my memories?'

'What do you want to remember?'

The ache in my foot sped up my leg and squatted inside my skull. 'The first fourteen years of my life.'

'I'll try,' she said.

She reached out to me, her fingers warm to the touch, pushing through my hair and resting on my head. She moved them across my flesh, a massage to retrieve what I'd lost so long ago. There was a crescendo of crashing noises and angry shouting outside the room, the other Ursula releasing her anger for the indignities performed on her unconscious body. She banged against the door and screamed. My skull throbbed as this Ursula gazed deep into my eyes, my mind swimming inside hers and vice versa.

We stood together like that for an eternity, our minds connected as she searched for my missing memories. My reflexes told me to resist and fight against the invasion, but I ignored them and let her enter my thoughts. As I did, I caught a glimpse of Ursula's older memories, of her as a child running across the sand as the sea caressed her toes. I felt the wind brushing against her hair, smelt the breeze in the air, and shivered as the cold water covered my feet. It was a beautiful day, and the sun's warmth kissed my skin. This was Ursula as a six-year-old, the one I'd met at the lake before her life sped into a downward spiral.

Then an electric spasm shot through my body and hers, pushing us apart like shooting stars crashing into each other before hurtling away. I plummeted to the floor, hitting my damaged ankle again and flinching with new pain. She reached to me and dragged me up.

'What did you find?'

Ursula grimaced and shook her head. 'I'm afraid Diana took those memories from you. You must see her about them.'

She disappeared before I could react. I froze in space, motionless inside her memories. I scanned the library and the books staring back at me.

Was I a novel without a beginning or end?

Then the angry Ursula crashed through the door, her eyes burning red as she leapt at me.

Chapter 12

Ruby's Diary

Day Five Hundred and Sixty-Six, Year Two

Earth Time: July 7, 1947. Location: Corona, New Mexico, USA. (Planet Earth).

The desert stretched as far as the eye could see. The sun beat down mercilessly on the dry, cracked earth, baking it to a deep red colour. The sky was a brilliant shade of blue, with no cloud in sight. The only thing that broke the monotony of the landscape was the occasional cactus or Joshua tree.

'Is there a good reason you've brought me here?' I said to Diana.

She removed her sunglasses and smiled at me. 'I told you earlier, this is important for you to know.'

The sweat poured down my face as the sun burnt my skin. I took a sip from my water bottle, but it was already warm. The desert was not completely barren. Small shrubs and cacti were scattered throughout the landscape, with the occasional lizard or snake darting across our path. The large birds circling above us appeared to be vultures waiting for their lunch.

We marched through rocks and boulders, some as little as pebbles and others as massive as cars. I had to be careful where I stepped, as the ground was unstable and could give way at any moment. A fine layer of dust and sand swirled around my feet with every step.

'Couldn't we have just used the Time Rings to get to our destination?'

She stopped, and I leaned against a huge rock, the heat seeping through my shirt and onto my arm. Above us, the vultures seemed to be getting closer.

'This is important, Ruby, because there might come a time when you don't have access to a Time Ring.'

I took a deep breath and stared at her. 'Have the Watchers rejected me?'

'Why would you say that?'

I slid into the shade of the rock. 'Because of what you said about the Time Ring.'

She shook her head. 'This is only a precautionary measure in case anything goes wrong. You need to know where I keep my personal acquisitions.'

She put her hand on the rock, and it vibrated enough to shake me off. I stumbled from it as a crack opened in the middle. Diana stepped through it, and I followed. Lights flickered on to illuminate the way as the gap closed behind me.

'Acquisitions?'

The air was thick with damp earth and the faint scent of burnt dust on the illuminations.

'Yes, the library isn't big enough to store everything I need, so I've dotted stuff around the universe. This is the first place I'll show you, but there are many more.'

As I walked, I noticed small pools of water collecting on the ground, their surfaces rippling with the echoes of my steps. The walls were slick with moisture, with little streams of liquid trickling down from unseen cracks above. The fluorescent lights flickered overhead, casting an eerie glow on the scene. The shadows danced and shifted on the surfaces, almost as if they were alive.

When we reached the end, I emerged into a large underground chamber filled with the hum of generators and the blinding light of flood lamps. The surface's fresh air and bright light were replaced by the corridor's damp, musty smell and flickering lights.

And then I saw the craft ahead of us.

'Is that...?'

Diana nodded. 'Yes, it's the ship I used to collect you from Saltburn in 1882. First, I must show you how to operate it.'

I walked up to the entrance, remembering how my life had changed the first time I stepped inside it.

'That's great, Diana, and I'm looking forward to it, but why would I need to fly this or anything like it when I have a Time Ring?'

She stopped at the door to the craft. 'Let's forget for a second about how many times I've warned you that there's no guarantee you'll have that Ring forever. So what would you do if you needed to move a living thing from one place to another in an emergency?'

I peered into her eyes. 'What type of emergency? I'm not supposed to change history, remember?'

Diana waved her hand at the craft, and the door opened. 'You need to be prepared for anything.'

I followed her inside, seeing nothing had changed since the last time I was there.

'Do the other Watchers know about this?'

She turned the control panel on and indicated for me to sit near her. So I did.

'No, Ruby, they don't. Things are changing within the Watchers that I can't go into detail about, but we must have a means for travel outside the Time Rings.'

The heat increased in my veins. 'Are you in trouble?'

She shook her head and smiled. 'Of course not. Now let's get started.'

I followed her instructions and focused on what I needed to learn, yet one thought possessed me.

Was I in trouble with the Watchers?

Two hours later, Diana pressed several buttons for the rock to open in the ceiling, taking the craft outside. The hairs on my arms stood on end as we drifted silently above the desert. She handled the controls for thirty seconds before looking at me.

'It's your turn.'

I didn't move from my seat, glued to the material as I viewed the screen showing the display outside.

'Are you sure?' I said.

Diana nodded. 'You'll be fine, Ruby. You can't do anything wrong.'

She moved her hands from the panel, and I placed my fingers above it, doing what she'd shown me to raise the craft higher and move it forward. It was like playing the theremin, manipulating electromagnetic fields by shifting my hands over the controls.

I saw us moving over the desert through the screen, and it felt great.

'Where are we going?' I said.

Before she could reply, the display fizzled in and out of focus.

Then a flash of lightning lit up the sky and smashed into us. It tilted to the side, and I went with it, tumbling out of the seat and crashing to the floor. My shoulder hit it first, shooting a bolt of pain through my arm and into the rest of me. Next, the craft twisted in the air, and I rolled into the wall, thumping into it with my other arm.

Another massive shock jolted us, sending all the lights on the control panel into overdrive. I clung to the nearest chair as we tumbled and spun into a dive towards the desert.

'We're going to crash!' Diana shouted. 'Return to the library ten minutes after we left.' I didn't move, the descent turning my guts into mush. 'Now, Ruby!'

'What about you?' I yelled.

She let go of her seat and slid across the floor, stopping next to me. Then she grabbed my hand.

'We leave together, right?'

I nodded.

Then we vanished.

Chapter 13

Casting the Runes

'Wake up, Ruby.'
          I returned to the land of the living as Dash leant over me with a wet cloth glued to my cheek.

'Pffff.' I blew the liquid from my face and sat up. 'No need to soak me in water to revive me, Dash.'

'This wasn't my doing, my friend. You're sweating like Niagara Falls.'

She threw me another towel as I got to my feet. I grabbed it and touched my wrist. The heat on my skin was uncomfortable, yet I felt nothing inside.

'I need a drink.'

'What happened?'

She handed me a glass of iced water. It swam down my throat and chilled my insides. Energy returned to me as I told her what had occurred with the versions of Ursula. I repeated everything apart from what I'd discovered about Diana's last experiment. It was something that couldn't just be blurted out until I got my mind around it.

'Those people, those so-called Queens of Heaven, revelled in what they did to her.'

I grasped for the image of Ishtar in my head, but all I retrieved was a blurred picture of the woman.

'Are you sure it was all real?'

Dash's question threw my scrambled concentration out of sync.

'What do you mean?'

'What if it wasn't a memory you accessed but some form of a dream or wish fulfilment?'

The hairs all along my arms prickled, irritating me, so I scratched at the symbols on my wrists, first one, then the other.

'Who would wish experiments on themselves?'

Dash struggled for an answer. 'Maybe it's another false memory, like they implanted in you.'

By they, she meant Diana.

I tried to shake the buzzing from my skull, but it only worsened. Had I volunteered for the same experiments they'd performed on Ursula and then lost that memory? Invisible weights constrained me as I considered the question, my flesh and bones pressing together to squeeze the breath from me.

'I need a shower.'

I headed to my room. The 1940s version wasn't that

different from the twenty-first century, besides having less dust and discarded clothes. And all the pulp magazines were brand new and not vintage.

Dash stood in the doorway. 'Why would Diana take your childhood memories from you?'

It was a question I'd asked myself a thousand times since Ursula mentioned it, and I was no closer to an answer. Or the answers I had were ones I didn't want to hear. Maybe my mind hadn't been wiped without my consent; what if it had been my idea? What if all of this was my doing?

That thought sent cramps through the whole of me. My legs turned to lead, and I used the wall for support.

Was I the architect of all my problems?

No, I refused to believe that. And I didn't think Diana had betrayed Ursula or me. My friend must have had good reasons for doing what she did, and I needed to find her again to discover what they were. But it still wasn't an easy thought to stomach.

Thinking about Diana's actions created a considerable weight in the pit of my gut. She'd kept countless things from me, and I hated her for that duplicity. No, I hated what she'd done; I could never hate her.

Dash stared at me, the fur on her face standing on end. The irony of looking at the person I'd hidden so many secrets from, including the events surrounding her death, filled me with guilt. Could I blame Diana for what she did, considering how I'd treated Dash all this time?

'You keep our guests company while I get cleaned up, and I'll see you soon.'

I needed the water to wash over me, wanting its pressure to sweep away the cobwebs of indecision invading my brain. Dash nodded and vanished. I pressed my head against the wall, and a monsoon of doubts crashed down. Was I ready to face the answers to my hidden past? I threw off my clothes and climbed into the shower. It was cold at first, freezing me as I shivered. I increased the temperature, so the steam engulfed me, and nothing but white clouds floated around.

A cavalcade of memories unfolded from me, images of Diana as my teacher, friend, and surrogate mother. I raised my arms out of the mist and stared at the lines on my wrists. Did the Watchers place something inside me during those experiments? What did those marks, and the ones on my back, represent? I'd always thought they looked like points on a connector or a socket. Maybe the Watchers intended to plug me into something. Was it possible there was no significance to my life beyond what they did, that I was only a conduit for what they needed to store or use?

Whatever it was they did, Gloriana's ability to travel through time and space without wearing a Time Ring proved they'd succeeded with at least one of their experiments. My fingers were close to my face, the Time Ring glistening in the water. It was a simple piece of silver, nothing special beyond what it did. I slipped it from my finger and placed it in the palm of my hand.

'I could drop you down the drain and be done with this forever.'

I spoke to it as if the Ring was human, as if it was Diana or my parents, with me waiting for a reprimand or a telling-off for being so foolish. I could stay in 1940 and spend my days talking to Ursula. Or I could hop back to live with Lucy and Daisy, give everything up, forget about my past and concentrate on the future. Wasn't that what Daisy said, to focus on the future and not dwell on the past or present?

That's how muddled I'd become, to be taking life lessons from a ten-year-old.

I climbed out of the shower and went to my emergency stash of clothes: a shirt, a jacket, and jeans were all I needed, with my favourite shoes. It was comforting to step into footwear that had stridden across alien landscapes and rested under Helen of Troy's bed. I glanced at Ursula as I vanished, remembering the beat of her heart and those familiar marks on her body.

Dash was making a pot of tea when I arrived. The look of surprise on my face must have worried her.

'I'm giving up the booze,' she said. I dropped into a comfy chair, not knowing what to say. 'I need a clear head for what comes next.'

I stayed silent. I'd known Dash to defeat a horde of barbarians while hung over and save Elvis's life after a twenty-four-hour bender. Excessive alcohol had never been a barrier to her doing what was necessary.

I glanced around the room. 'Where are our guests?'

'They went up top to gaze at the stars.'

'That sounds like a good idea; we should join them.'

It had been so long since I'd looked at something and not wondered what it would be like if I changed it.

'Okay,' Dash said. 'I'll meet you up there.'

I put my hand on her arm before she disappeared. 'No. Let's go up in the lift.'

She narrowed her eyes, the fur bristling on her face. 'Well, this makes a change.' She took my wrist and led me to the lift. There was so much I needed to tell her, but I didn't know where to begin. The elevator was as I remembered it; metallic and cold. Dash must have sprayed air freshener inside it because it smelt of strawberries. It would only take a few minutes to reach the top. 'So, what do you want to talk about?'

I could keep secrets from her, but I could never fool her. So I plucked the diagrams from my memory. 'Ursula showed me the last thing Diana worked on for the Queens: a self-contained, perpetual time loop.'

Her eyes grew large and wide. 'What does this time loop do?'

The schematics and information from Ursula's mind glared at me inside my head.

'You remember I told you Gloriana said all of us are ageing, even if it's at a reduced pace?'

She laughed as we neared the top. 'The hardships these poor Watchers have to endure.'

I grinned with her. The tiny sliver of joy rippling through me was a relief from the millions of things in my brain.

'Indeed,' I said. We were close to the exit when Dash hit the button to pause our journey.

She peered at me. 'When I was a kid, about the age Daisy is now, my father always complained about his lot in life; about the job he hated, the type of house he could afford, about his lack of social status. Then, when he'd had enough to drink, he would moan about marrying the wrong woman and putting up with his ungrateful brat of a child.' Dash looked at me through the most sorrowful eyes I'd ever seen. I'd spent so much time worrying about my lost childhood I'd never thought what hers must have been like. 'He was never happy, no matter what he had, no matter what he did, even though he was better off than eighty percent of the planet.' She set the lift moving again. 'These Watchers remind me of him.'

I didn't know what to say. I had no point of reference

for dealing with parents, good or bad. I had my memories of Diana, of how she was what I perceived a mother to be. But those memories were tainted now, doubts creeping in about whether they were real. All I could do was hold Dash's paw to feel her warm fur tickling my skin.

'I saw the data on the computer screen in Ursula's memory. Those who wear the Time Rings are ageing, and it's worse for those who've worn them the longest.'

The lift came to a halt with a thump. 'Why is that, Ruby?'

I shrugged. 'I'm not sure, but from what Ursula remembered from Diana's notes, she thought it might be because long-term contact with the Time Ring technology could negatively affect the wearer's DNA.'

'Does this internal time device block that from happening?'

I shook my head. 'This was why Diana experimented with time loops, to see if she could stop or reverse the process.'

We stepped into the night as a chill wind caressed the marks on the back of my neck.

'And did she discover this?'

'No, but she found something else.'

A small bundle of energy whacked into my legs as I finished speaking.

'It's Ruby and Dash, partners in time.'

Daisy grabbed my arm and dragged me towards the stones. She let go of my hand and skipped between each obelisk with her mother in hot pursuit. She danced around them as if she was back in the playground. I tilted my face upwards and peered into the stars, glittering so close. I lifted my fingers above my head, the tips getting near those celestial objects.

Dash joined me. 'So what does a time loop do?'

I gazed into the radiance sparkling above us. 'According to Diana's notes, it contains time inside one specified location, while everything continues outside it as we advance towards entropy. Theoretically, those in the loop would never age.'

'Wouldn't they be frozen?' Daisy's words surprised me. Lucy smiled as if her daughter's grasp of complex concepts was an everyday occurrence.

I answered the kid's question. 'No, Daisy; that's the beauty of it. They can live inside the loop while the rest of the world moves forward.'

Imprinted on my mind was the computer screen filled with Diana's theory.

'Sounds like a terrible boring bubble to live in,' Daisy said before she skipped into the centre of the stones.

'What would the Watchers want these time loops for?' Dash said.

I could only think of one thing. 'It would make a perfect prison.' I dropped to the ground and lay on my back to gaze into the sky. 'Diana must be inside one of these time loops. But how do we find it and her?'

Dash shrugged, jumped over me and scampered towards Daisy, a pensive look overtaking her face.

'Daisy's a child prodigy,' Lucy Lynx said as she joined me. 'Her teachers keep telling me she could go to university now, even to Oxford or Cambridge, but it doesn't feel right for a ten-year-old. So what would you do?'

I didn't know how to reply. Sending a ten-year-old to university seemed troubling, but I didn't want to offend Lucy by saying the wrong thing. Even though Daisy played with Dash in the stones, I knew she could overhear us. I smiled and left Lucy to continue.

'I know you're clever, Ruby; were you always studying when you were young?'

She peered at me, and it took all my willpower to stop wishing I was somewhere else. How could I tell her I had no memory of that age because my friend, my surrogate mother, had stolen that time from me?

Before I considered escaping, Daisy jumped on top of me with such a thump she knocked the wind from my lungs.

'Daisy,' her mother shouted. It had no discernible effect as the kid thrust her fingers into my side to tickle the flesh from my bones.

'Oh-oh,' Dash said. 'The kid's started a war she can never win.'

I let Daisy get the first few licks in before I twisted my hips and deposited her on the ground. Then I pushed my hands under her arms and tickled until she cried surrender. We ended up side by side, peering at the speckles of light above and laughing as I'd never done before. Once again, I thought about throwing the Ring away and starting a new life. Once again, I wondered if my parents had played with me like this.

Dash picked Daisy up and rubbed her hairy nose against the kid's face. They laughed together before Dash dropped her back to the ground.

'Daisy, where would you go if you could live anywhere in the world?'

I guessed it was Dash's subtle approach to get mother and daughter out of our dangerous lives, but I wasn't sure if I wanted that anymore. The kid had more energy than rocket fuel, leaping up and glueing herself to Dash's waist.

'Anywhere with you and Ruby!' Daisy shouted.

It made my heart flutter, but I knew it couldn't happen.

I rubbed my thumb against the Ring on my finger.

'How did you get that?' Lucy said as Daisy and Dash played "Ring a Ring o' Roses."

'My friend gave it to me.'

A flash of memory rippled back into my consciousness.

'These are for you,' Diana had told me as red lights and sirens went off all around us. I'd spent many years searching my brain for reasons why she'd never left with me. Had she stayed behind as a sacrifice to keep me safe, or was it all some ploy for something else? I found it difficult to reconcile the good we'd had with the lies and the memory theft. It didn't matter what I did – my mind kept flip-flopping between wondering if Diana had betrayed me or saved me.

Or perhaps letting me go was only another experiment, so she and the others had been observing me ever since. It would explain why they'd never come looking for me. And it didn't bear thinking about.

'That woman who saved me from the car accident has this thing inside her?' Lucy's voice trembled, on the verge of breaking down at the memory of a death she never had.

'That woman is called Gloriana, and that's what she claims. But, of course, she could have been lying about that.' I doubted every single word Gloriana said.

Lucy scrutinised me. 'Will you do the same thing to yourself?'

'Wait. What?' I stuttered.

'I suppose it would be dangerous, but then those men searching for you wouldn't recognise you from the Ring on your hand.'

'No, not that.' The palpitations in my chest were like a mini heart attack. 'You said Gloriana saved you from the accident? I thought there was no accident.'

'What's wrong?' Dash heard my rising voice, so she sat

next to me.

'Lucy, what happened with you and Gloriana?' I said.

Daisy joined us, so we all sat in the middle of Stonehenge. We were somewhere in the mark the builders had left thousands of years ago, and we spoke about impossible things.

Lucy was nervous, her fingers shaking as she recalled meeting Gloriana. 'The car headed straight for me. I was frozen in the road when she stepped out in front, and the driver slammed on the brakes.'

'Didn't we already know this?' Dash said.

I ignored the question. 'Then what happened?'

Lucy stared at her daughter. 'The woman grabbed my hand, and we disappeared. It went dark, and I panicked before reappearing at my house. Men were lying on the floor. She said they were dead, and if I didn't do as I was told, the same thing would happen to Daisy. Then she took me to that café, and I met you.'

The memory of it brought tears to her eyes.

Daisy reached over to console her. 'Don't worry, Mum; everything's okay now.'

Heat burst from Dash's face as she fumed. 'What sort of game is this Gloriana playing?'

Anger blinded her to the most important thing Lucy had said.

'She took you through time and space twice?' I said to Lucy.

'Yes, I think so,' she replied as Daisy gripped her fingers.

'Damn!' Dash said. 'That means...'

'Gloriana can take others with her when she travels, even if they don't have a Time Ring.'

Dash and I gazed at each other.

This would change everything.

Chapter 14

The Science of Time

D ash's fur bristled as her eyes bulged. 'Gloriana transported you with her through time and space?'

Lucy nodded. 'I don't know about time travelling, but she took me from one place to another in an instant.'

'How did she do it?' I said.

'She grabbed my hand, and then we vanished. The first time, I was still shocked from seeing that car driving towards me.'

Her voice trembled as she spoke, and I peered deep into her eyes. She was holding something back about her near-death experience with the hit-and-run, but I would not push her about it. Not now and not with Daisy there. But there was more I needed to know.

'What did it feel like?'

Lucy took a deep breath. 'All the hair on my arms stood on end, and a great heat swept through me. My whole body vibrated like a rollercoaster, and a rainbow of colours covered my eyes. Then, when we arrived at my house, I had to sit for a minute to calm down.' She glanced between Dash and me. 'Is it like that for you when you travel through space or time?'

Dash shook her head. 'No. It's a perfectly normal experience.' She gazed at me. 'Unless we journey too close to a previous point we've travelled from. Then things get a little tricky.'

Daisy jumped up like a jack-in-the-box. 'I want to do that.' She threw her arms around her mother. 'Can I be a time traveller, Mum?'

I watched Lucy whisper into her daughter's ear, trying to control Daisy's excitement when it would have been easier to stop a hurricane from blowing you over. I left them to it and sidled up to Dash.

'This could change everything for us.'

Having the technology inside the body didn't just allow that person to travel through space and time: they could take others with them.

Now that was groundbreaking.

She agreed. 'I can see why they were keen for Diana to continue her experiments.'

Daisy and Lucy separated, and the kid had the biggest smile on her face.

'Mum says we'll live with you and have adventures in time and space.'

Lucy Lynch gasped. 'Daisy, that's not what I said.'

Daisy spoke a thousand words a minute, like an overexcited typewriter come to life. I didn't pay attention and peered at my hands. I scratched at the marks on my wrists as mother and daughter stopped talking, and we digested the enormity of this news. We sat there in stunned silence, stars twinkling above us as fireworks erupted inside me. I turned to Dash.

'You need to perform the surgery on me.'

She looked at me aghast, shaking her head so hard I thought most of her fur would blow away in the wind. 'That's crazy, Ruby. We don't know what might happen.'

'You're a doctor.'

'Not for humans.'

'I watched the procedure in Ursula's memory. I remember it and can talk you through it. All we have to do is straighten this out.'

I had the Ring in the palm of my hand, grateful I hadn't thrown it away earlier. It felt like any other metal, cold against my skin, but it seemed to hum to me. I'd always assumed that the technology manipulated vibrational frequencies somehow, shifting the wearer through wormholes so they could travel through space and time. It worked as a transmitter linked to an individual's DNA so the brain could connect to any point in space and time. Diana had never explained how it functioned, but I'd picked up tiny bits of knowledge about it during my brief life with her. So now, if the device was inside the body, the traveller could use physical contact with others to take them through time and space.

'You said it didn't work on Ursula.'

'I assume that was because Diana was trying it through the wrists.' I raised my fingers to my neck and remembered what Ishtar had said in Ursula's memory. 'It must be done through the spine, directly connecting to the brain.'

This was all guesswork, but I knew it to be true.

'Then why didn't she do it to you before she helped you escape?'

'She probably couldn't risk my life. Maybe the experiments Ursula underwent were what caused those anomalies in her brain. Diana wouldn't want that for me.' I recalled the power in Ishtar's voice. 'But I guess the Queens of Heaven pressurised her to continue her tests on younger subjects.'

Terror possessed Dash's face. But she knew I couldn't give up on this idea. And we both understood how dangerous it would be.

'What are you saying, Ruby?'

'Diana had to try it on herself first. Perhaps the Queens had wanted to experiment with me, so she helped me escape.'

She had saved me. Everything she'd done was to protect me. I still couldn't understand why she'd removed and altered my memories, but she'd got me away from the Queens of Heaven and the Watchers to protect me.

'If Diana thought the procedure was too dangerous for you, why do you want to do it now?'

I held up my hands so she could see the marks on my wrists. 'Things are different now, Dash. Consider what I might do with the technology inside me.' I nodded toward Daisy and her mother. 'I could take them anywhere to start new lives. Once we know it works on me, you could have the same operation, then think how many more people we could save.' I touched her paw, feeling her fur bristle. 'We could even return to Avon and save all those who died in that quake.'

I didn't mention returning to Felineous to save her family and friends, but I assumed she must have also thought about it.

She snatched her arm from me. 'Is this just another way for you to become God?' Anger seeped out of her, but I recognised it was through fear of what might happen to me. 'You sound like one of these Queens of Heaven, Ruby. All this power is going to your head.' She gripped her claws into her palms, jumped up, and stormed away.

'You two think about where you want to live,' I said to mother and daughter as I sprang to my feet and sprinted after Dash. The wind chilled my skin as I ran past the stones and caught up with her on the far side.

'We'll need every advantage if we move forward with this, Dash.'

She refused to look me in the eye. 'If?'

'Yes. We don't need to find Diana; we'll ignore Gloriana's warnings and do whatever we want. It would be easy to go back to the life we had or start a new one. If I have the Time Ring technology inside me, we can take Daisy and Lucy with us.'

It all sounded so tempting.

She turned to me. 'You would do that, sacrifice your friend and any hope you have of finding your parents and recovering your memories?'

Moisture dripped into the hairs on her cheek.

'I will for you.'

The Moon appeared from nowhere and bathed us in its silvery glow. We held each other, tears flowing from both sides until we separated.

'And what happens when they come for us, Ruby? You know there's more to this than we're aware of. All those hints and warnings from Gloriana mean something.'

'I understand that. So the more choices we have, the better prepared we'll be for when the attack comes.' My fingers touched her fur. 'And that's why I need you to do this for me, to put the Time Ring inside my body.'

'And you're sure about this?'

I gripped her paws. 'I am.'

Dash pushed a stray hair from my head. 'At the first sign of trouble, I'm calling it off.'

'Of course.'

We stood in complete silence for what seemed like forever. The stars shimmered above us as the wind whistled between the stones.

'When do you want to do it, Ruby?'

'You need to operate as soon as possible. But there are things I have to tell you first. No more secrets.'

She narrowed her eyes at me. 'Why? Because you think you might not survive the operation?'

I tightened my grip on her, trying to stop her from wavering. 'No, it's nothing to do with that. There are important matters I've kept from you, and I'm sorry. It won't happen again, I promise.'

So I told her about Gloriana and Gideon's fragments in time theory. She didn't seem surprised by it.

'I've always thought our changes would have more consequences than we saw, so it sounds feasible.' She glanced at the stones. 'Imagine all those different versions of Daisy existing somewhere.'

I tried not to think about Daisy with half of her face missing or dying at the hands of her terrible father. And I still had my doubts about Gloriana's claim.

'But they have no proof.'

'You know it must be likely. Otherwise, you wouldn't have gone through the charade of Lucy's funeral.'

Dash was right, but it was a puzzle for another day. If I was giving up my secrets to this night, then there was one more I had to unburden myself from.

'There's something else I must tell you.'

'Okay,' she said.

'It's about your death.'

The colour drained from her fur. 'I don't need to know.'

But I needed to tell her before the guilt consumed me. 'You wondered how I changed the Ring, so it works for you.' She was a doctor but no scientist, so I'd always baffled her with some gobbledygook. 'The device needs tuning to your DNA, so I had to switch from human biology to yours.'

'I understand,' she replied. 'You've told me this before.'

Tension strained her voice and my heart. 'But I never mentioned how I did it.'

I hadn't told her how I became Dr Frankenstein.

Dash put her paw on my arm. 'You don't have to do this, Ruby.'

But I did, more than ever.

'I needed part of your brain to recode the DNA sequence, part of the brain which wasn't working anymore.'

Tears slipped down my cheeks. I couldn't say the rest, but she knew what I meant.

Her lips trembled. 'You removed it from me when I took an overdose.'

I stared at her and remembered Felineous, pictured the terrible thing I'd done to save her, to save a version of her.

'I did. Immediate cold storage was imperative. So I left you on the floor.' It was a memory buried deep into the abyss inside me until now. 'I was too late when I returned the first time, but it helped because....'

'You took some of my brain from the dead version of me

132

so you could use it when you went back again and saved me on your second go.'

I wiped my face and nodded. After keeping this dreadful secret for so long, I'd always thought the version of Dash I'd cut open would have blinked out of existence when I went back the second time and saved her. But now, maybe there was still that fragment of her somewhere with her brains spilt onto the floor. The image raced through my memories, trying to undo all the good times we'd shared.

'I had to make an incision at the base of your cerebellum, cut out a small piece and replace it with the matter from the other version of you.'

I was Dr Frankenstein, indeed.

'Are you a scientist, Ruby?' I shook my head. 'Are you a doctor?'

'You know I'm not.'

'Then how were you able to change the DNA structure of the Time Ring?'

'I just did.' It had come naturally to me, like second nature.

'How did you know which parts of my brain needed altering?'

'I just did.' I'd never doubted myself, neither then nor now.

'Did Diana replace your memories with other ones?'

'What do you mean?'

'There must be a reason she gave you two Time Rings when she knew she couldn't escape with you.'

I'd always assumed she was coming with me but had given me an extra Ring when she realised she couldn't get away.

'You think she intended to give it to me so I could have someone to travel with?'

'It's possible. She wouldn't have wanted you to be alone. And maybe she placed the knowledge to change the Time Ring inside your head.'

She'd manipulated my mind again. But for my benefit. I tried to shake the deception from my skull, both Diana's and my duplicity.

'Do you forgive me?'

I couldn't forgive myself for keeping this from her all this time.

Dash smiled and grabbed me, going through another round of hugs before coming up for air.

'There's nothing to forgive, my friend. You did what you had to do to save me.' She raised her hand to look at the Time Ring. 'And you made it possible for this to work for me. I'll always be grateful for that. Now let's rescue Diana.'

A great weight lifted from me as we walked back to find Daisy and Lucy deep in conversation. I wondered if they were deciding on somewhere new to live.

'I'll assist you with your operation,' Lucy said, to my surprise. Dash whistled and winked at the kid. I could only stand there and look dumbfounded. 'I'm a trained nurse, didn't you know?'

Dash grinned at me as I shook my head. It appeared as if everything was falling into place.

I removed the Ring. 'We need to flatten this out.'

'Aren't you scared you might break it?' It had to be Daisy who voiced my fear.

I ruffled her hair. 'It'll be fine, kid.'

I'd contemplated walking away from this life, so what difference did it make if I lost it all through my recklessness? That thought consumed me all the way down in the lift.

Dash went to the workshop. 'I'll get the tools.'

My part-time work as a blacksmith in Pompeii was

about to be of use. To the best of my knowledge and experience, the Ring couldn't be destroyed, but it was malleable enough to be modified, which meant it could be damaged if I got it wrong. So it was one more worry at the back of my mind.

I went to the makeshift forge at the rear of the base while Dash prepared the medical equipment. It didn't take long for the furnace to reach the right temperature, with the heat making the sweat drip from my forehead. Then I placed the Time Ring inside the furnace and watched it change colour as the temperature increased. Finally, the Ring glowed, first red, then orange, then yellow. That's when I knew it was ready. I lifted the hammer when Daisy spoke from the doorway.

'What happens if you break it, and it won't work anymore?'

As I looked at her, the hammer was heavy in my hand, the heat making me sweat even more.

'It will be fine, Daisy. Now go back to the others and see if they need help.'

She gazed at me, not as a child would, but as if she was an adult, understanding that what I was about to do would change everything for all of us.

Then she left.

And I brought down the hammer onto the Time Ring.

Everything I'd ever done with the technology, all my adventures since escaping from the Watchers, flashed through my mind. But as the temperature increased inside and outside of me, I pushed all the doubts away. I left it to cool down when I finished and did the same. I'd flattened the Time Ring into perfection, and the humming noise had vanished.

Had I destroyed it after all?

When the heat dissipated, I took it to Dash. She showed me the pills in her paw.

'I brought the extra strong sedatives.'

'No need,' I replied. 'I have to describe the procedure to you, so I'll be awake while you do it. You must restrain my arms.'

'Wait in Ruby's room,' Dash said to Daisy, but the kid ignored her. She was as stubborn as me. Dash had the scalpel in her hand while Lucy fastened the belts around my wrists. She took the flattened Time Ring from me. 'I have no idea what to do with this once I make the incision.'

'I think it will find its own way if connected to my DNA.' That's what I hoped.

'I'll miss the pretty ring.'

Daisy didn't appreciate the magnitude of what was about to happen, which was a good thing as there was no need to worry her. The table was cold against my shoulders as I removed my top.

Fear crept into Dash's voice. 'Are you sure you don't want any painkillers?'

'My body needs to be awake for the metal to graft onto it.' At least, that's what I believed.

Lucy peered at the material Dash was holding. 'How does it work if that's only a normal piece of metal?'

'Magic,' Daisy said as Dash laid the squashed Ring next to me. My chin dug into the table as the blade touched my back.

'If I get this wrong, you could end up paralysed.'

'Then don't get it wrong,' I said as the scalpel cut into my skin.

Chapter 15

The Clock of the Heart

I tried to steady my breathing as I peered at the ceiling. The muffled voices dragged my attention back to those with me in the room, and I smiled at Daisy and Lucy as they gazed at me. They attempted to hide their tension, but it wasn't easy. My heart pounded in my chest, and I pictured how the universe's history would open up for us if this succeeded. I closed my eyes and thought of Diana and Ursula. When the idea for the operation came to me, about twenty seconds after I realised the importance of Lucy's words, I told myself I'd risk it to save my friends. Yet, deep down, I knew there was also another reason: I wanted to know what that power would feel like, the ability to take others with me through space and time.

'Are you ready, Ruby?'

I opened my eyes and nodded to Dash. 'Slice away, my friend.'

She didn't hesitate and cut along the dark line tattooed on the back of my neck. The blade was cold, and so was the trickle of blood that dribbled down my skin. An aroma of burnt copper assaulted my senses. Silver kissed my flesh, and my fingers trembled. I pressed my chin hard into the table underneath me, desperate to squeeze out the tension in my muscle and bone.

'Are you sure you're okay, Ruby?' She tried to keep the strain from her voice, but it didn't work.

'Don't worry, Dash; this won't take long.'

I pictured the scene I'd witnessed in Ursula's memory. The cut had been along her wrist and not the neck, but I remembered how Diana placed the metal inside the incision. That's all Dash needed to do once she got under my skin. On the table to my right sat the Time Ring I'd flattened a short while ago.

One thought rattled around my skull on a constant loop. What if I'd damaged the internal mechanisms of the device under the heat? If I had, and it didn't work, I'd be stuck in this time zone forever, to age again like a normal person.

But would that be such a terrible thing?

My thoughts evaporated as the knife cut into me again as she extended the opening. My heart rate increased, my hands clenched as stabs of pain jumped from my back and sped through me, veins, muscles and bones vibrating as if about to explode. I ground my teeth while trying to keep still. One move from me and Dash could slip and slice into my spine. Lucy wiped the sweat from my head, her breath caressing my face. The smell of the antiseptic was sickeningly sweet.

'Okay, I've finished the incision.' The scalpel clattered onto the table as Dash dropped it. 'Lucy will pull the skin back now.'

We'd spoken about this beforehand. Lucy was reluctant to stick her hand into my blood and bits, even as a trained nurse, but we told her it would be impossible for Dash to do it using her paws. Only when Daisy offered to help did her mother agree.

Lucy's fingers trembled as she touched me. She pushed them down a little, and they nipped against my skin. Her hands were cold, but I was on fire. I ground my teeth even further and resisted the urge to scream. Instead, I focused on the smell of my blood, that fragrance of seared metal that drifted up my nose and made my eyes water. I wanted to rub my face to clear my vision but couldn't because of the restraints. The thumping inside my skull grew louder, pounding against my brain until I heard the beating of my heart coursing through me. But then another noise appeared, the sound of Daisy speaking to me.

'Don't worry, Ruby; you'll be okay.'

Her words calmed me, even though every inch of me was on fire. Lucy's fingers pushed further into my back, making room for the flattened Time Ring. I stared at the floor, seeing this exact scene, but with Ursula in my place and Diana cutting into her. She'd got me away from the Queens of Heaven so I wouldn't have to suffer this procedure, yet here I was volunteering for it.

I focused on that contradiction to soften the pain infecting me, but as Lucy worked in slow motion, the room shimmered around me, and everything vanished. I wasn't lying on the table anymore, but flat in the grass, the base under Stonehenge replaced by wind, rain, and cliffs. Water splattered against my hair as a stranger spoke to me.

'She jumped from this cliff, and we were helpless to do anything about it.'

It was a male voice I didn't recognise as a sea breeze swept into my head, an aroma of salt invading my senses. I couldn't move as something cold pressed against my spine. Fever possessed me as I shivered in that unknown place. Tension sparkled in the air as electric teeth formed from dark clouds threatened to cut into me. A bitter rain descended from the sky and sliced into my cheeks. I should have been staring at the floor in our base under Stonehenge, but somehow all I saw were gulls flying around me. They chattered and squawked, and I wanted to get up and run, but my legs wouldn't work.

The words tumbled out of my mouth. 'Who jumped?'

The stranger ignored my question. 'We need to make sure you don't have the same disease.'

Rough fingers grabbed me and pulled me backwards. I didn't want to go back, only forwards, always forwards. I turned and stared into burning red eyes.

'Set me free,' I shouted.

'I'll whip it out of you, child.'

His hands were large and cruel, his coarse skin cutting into mine. The sky had darkened, the wind replaced by icy rain battering my cheeks. It seeped into my face as the gulls swooped around my head, screeching and chattering as if they were talking to me.

'Let me go,' I howled.

His fingers dug deeper into my arms, drawing blood that swam down my skin.

'Do you know why she jumped?' he said.

I trembled in his grip. 'No.'

He pressed his face against mine, and I smelt the whisky on his breath.

'She was infected. You're all diseased; the only cure is to beat it out of you. Do you understand?'

I shook my head as my vision started to clear. 'Who are you?'

He didn't answer and threw me to the ground. I landed on my back, shock rippling through my spine and paralysing me. Then I looked up to see his vast shadow looming over me. And in his hand was the instrument of pain.

A scream died in my throat as the leather hit my face. The rain engulfed me, turning red as the blood seeped from my cheek. A gush of agony rushed through my sinew and bone. I tried to crawl away on my back, digging my nails into the dirt and dragging my body from him.

But I was slow, and he followed me all the way. Whenever his hand came down, he discovered a new spot to hit. Then, when he'd found every part of me, he started again, always saying the same thing as he struck.

'We have to beat out your disease.'

The rain soaked me but refused to wash away my blood and misery. I stopped moving when I reached the cliff edge, staring at his hand and seeing the cracked shell of his watch. Time had paused there, but not for me as he continued. The whip came again and again, slicing and cutting through my flesh until I could take it no more. And then the darkness collapsed upon me.

* * *

A surge of elephants stomped on my bones as I woke. I rolled onto my side and stared at Daisy sitting on the floor next to my bed.

'You've been swearing in your sleep,' the kid said. 'All sorts of naughty words my mum doesn't like.'

I dragged my aching body upwards and forced a smile. I reached out and touched her cheek. She was warm and full of life. A flash of memory punched into the back of my brain, of Daisy with only half a face. I swept the image away and beamed at her.

'Don't tell your mother or Dash.'

My legs found strength from somewhere and pushed me forwards. Daisy clutched at my fingers, and that strength increased tenfold. She was a battery recharging my weary flesh. But, in reality, it wasn't my body that suffered but my mind: the sweat dripped off me like a river, but all I could think about was that rain.

And the beating.

My bare feet dropped onto the cold floor, a spasm of ice running through my toes and ankles. I grabbed a towel from the back of the door and wiped my head. The kid and I left my room and went into the lounge to find Dash and Lucy in hushed conversation.

Concern engulfed Dash's face. 'How are you feeling?'

I dug my nails into my hand. 'Great.' Daisy must have sensed the anger building in me and ran to her mother. The wind, rain, cliff tops, and voice were back in my head. A flock of seagulls shrieked at me, but I knew they weren't there. 'What happened to me?'

I tried to push all those sounds and images away, wanting my memories to return, but not like this. Dash offered me a glass of water when I desperately needed something more substantial.

'You blacked out when I placed the Time Ring in your back.'

'Did you position it along my spine?'

She shook her head. 'I did nothing. It slithered into you like a snake. Then it disappeared into your blood.' She put the drink aside when she realised I didn't want it. 'Can you feel it inside you?'

My hand trembled as I moved it over my shoulder and stretched my fingertips for the wound. The scar was harsh against my flesh, but I couldn't feel anything underneath the skin. Instead, something else stabbed against my insides.

We'll whip it out of you, child, your disease.

I yelled at the voice in my head.

'We've been living in a bubble.' I threw the towel to the floor, my mind on fire and my limbs trembling.

Anxiety gripped Dash's face. 'What do you mean?'

'Daisy described the time loop as a bubble, which I've existed in since Diana set me free. I kept waiting for the Watchers to come after me, thinking I was so clever they'd never find me, but in reality, I wasn't important enough for them to bother.'

I was nothing to them, an abandoned experiment for the Queens of Heaven. So instead, they'd focused their attention on Diana, and I'd left my friend with them. This sudden realisation I wasn't as significant as I thought deflated me.

And the returning memories I'd been so desperate for were nothing but pain and anguish. Maybe that's why Diana had taken them from me – to save me from more suffering. No matter how terrible it seemed, all she'd done had been to protect me. And I'd let Diana down, leaving her to suffer with the Queens and what they were forcing her to do.

I needed something to occupy both my mind and body.

'We must test me to see if the operation worked. I have to take someone with me through space and time.'

A furred paw reached for my arm. 'Maybe you need to rest more; give your body time to adjust to the technology inside you. I got you to bed after you blacked out, but you said many strange things in your sleep.'

'What strange things?'

Concern consumed her face. 'Sometimes, you shouted out, saying you were....'

My heartbeat slowed until I could hardly feel it. 'What?'

'You said you were a disease that needed eliminating.' She gave me her best smile. 'It was probably the shock of the Time Ring attaching itself to your spine, that's all.'

Dr Dash tried her finest bedside manner to soothe my growing frustration. I pushed the cliff nightmare into the shadows of my mind and focused on what I had to do.

'There's no more time to waste.' I snatched the hooded top from the back of the chair and slipped it over my aching arms. 'We have to check if the operation worked.'

If it didn't, would we be able to retrieve the metal from inside me and get it to work as a functioning Time Ring again? Had all of this been my unconscious mind working in self-destruct mode? Even that nightmare?

'Take me,' Daisy shouted as she ran around the room. She grabbed an original model Spitfire from a shelf, stretched her arms out and turned into a human aeroplane.

'That won't happen, young lady.' Dash scowled, forgetting she wasn't the kid's mother. 'It might be dangerous for whoever Ruby takes.'

'What do you mean?' Lucy caught hold of Daisy before

she staggered into a pile of pop magazines from the 1980s. The kid twisted away from her mother.

Daisy stuck her hands out and buzzed around the room. 'It could be like *The Fly*.' She dived between the furniture before landing back in front of me. The three of us stared at her in confusion. 'You know, that old movie where the heads get switched in the transporter.' Daisy peered at us like we were rubes just stepping off the boat.

'Don't look at me,' Lucy said. 'It must have been her father letting her watch such nonsense.'

The mention of Dale Lynx irritated my skin. A phantom itch grew around the scar on my back.

'It's not nonsense,' Daisy said in a huff. 'Though I don't understand how both heads could have the man's brain. That made little sense.' She pursed her lips and gazed at the cobwebs hanging from the rafters. 'The man with the fly head can still think and do stuff like a person, but the fly with the human head can still talk.'

'I believe our child genius is trying to say that we don't know what will happen to the non-time travelling person you'll attempt to take with you. Their Bits could end up anywhere, even inside you,' Dash said.

'Oban transported us across the universe, from the Moon to Avon. We were okay.'

Dash grimaced. 'I remember it differently than you – it was an awful experience, so different to how we travel using the Time Rings.'

'Different technology, I suppose,' I said.

'What's an Oban?' Daisy said.

I ruffled her hair. 'I'll tell you when you're older. I have to test the technology stuck to my spine first.'

It didn't fill me with joy, but it was necessary.

'What's the rush?' Dash said.

'There was no point putting the Time Ring inside me if we won't use it.'

I understood her not wanting to test it on the kid, but we had to try it out with some living thing.

Dash came up with an idea. 'Go back in time and grab a small dinosaur.'

Daisy's eyes lit up at the mention of it. 'Yeah, get me a T-Rex to play with.'

She scrunched her face and stomped around the base like Godzilla, making enraged dinosaur noises.

I didn't like the concept. 'What if my going back with the technology inside me is what causes their extinction?'

The potential pitfalls were many and significant for the whole of the planet. And even the universe. So I needed to be less reckless than I usually was when travelling through space and time.

'Take a kitten with you,' Lucy said.

Dash growled at her, and she hung her head in apology.

'Take a sick person with you.' Daisy stopped pretending to be a dinosaur. 'Make someone who will die happy and take them somewhere wonderful.' The kid was damn mature for a ten-year-old, but I didn't like to tell her we would all die: even the immortals. 'Just like I died.'

Lucy's eyes dropped as she hugged her child. Did Daisy somehow remember what had happened to her in a previous timeline? Was this a fragmented memory? Could she recall her father pushing the steaming iron into her face or thrusting his fingers into her neck? I glanced at Dash and wondered if she had memories of her death on Felineous.

Perhaps there were no fragmented versions of people, only memory fragments lingering in the minds of those whose lives had changed. I didn't know which would be better.

'It's as good an idea as anything,' Dash said.

'I know the right person for it.' Lucy continued to squeeze the life from her daughter. 'At the hospital where I work, we have a ward for people with a terminal illness, including a man who has never seen his grandchildren who live on the other side of the world.'

She convinced me. 'Tell me his name, room number and the hospital.'

Lucy told me, and Dash went to the computer to find an image of the place.

But I had a better plan. 'No need, Dash. I'll try without.'

She stopped in surprise. 'You must visualise where you're going; it won't work otherwise.'

That was how we time-hopped and space-jumped before – we needed to have seen the location, even if it was only in a photo or video clip. The visualisation triggered the connection between the Time Ring and the brain. But it felt different now, with it clinging to my spine.

'I think it's changed because of the technology inside me.'

Lucy handed me a piece of paper. 'Here's the information you need.'

'Wish me luck.' I scanned the details before reaching into my mind for the trigger.

Hugh Little, ward two, room six, Mercy General.

My hands didn't tremble, but I felt something move along my spine.

Then I vanished.

Chapter 16

Ruby's Diary

Day Six Hundred and Sixty-Six, Year Two

Earth Time: Unknown. Location: Planet Deminaur.

A rush and a push and a shove.

I ran. I ran so far away.

'Take these.' Diana shoved the Time Rings and data communicators into my hands.

My lips trembled. 'You're not coming with me?'

'I can't, Ruby. If I leave with you, they'll look for us. This is the only way I can keep you safe.'

She touched my cheek, and then she was gone.

I was alone.

Again.

I set the data communicator to give me a random time and location and then pulled the trigger in my head.

Then I landed on Deminaur.

The smell hit me first; the stench of earth seeped in blood and guts, bones and sinew piled high across a corpse field. I heard the buzzing next, of the shadows hovering above me that weren't shadows but were thousands of flies filling their bellies. Above them were the birds that fed on death, circling and waiting for the living to depart. And I saw the living as well, the groups of people picking over the bodies. One dragged a corpse to the side, guts sliding out of the cavernous hole in the stomach, then reaching down to take the dead man's boots. I gazed beyond him, staring at the field of corpses, and wondered what had happened. Then something ran into me, knocking the wind from my sails as we crashed to the ground together.

'Get off me!' the girl shouted. Her arms were tangled in the bag on my shoulder as she twisted and turned to get loose. I resisted the urge to flick the trigger in my head and gripped her shoulders.

'Calm down, and I'll get you free.'

Her eyes blazed like an exploding sun as she scowled at me. She couldn't have been more than ten years old, dressed in rags, with a face covered in dirt. Several bruises added colour to her arms as she swore, some of which must have been a local dialect, as my translator failed to work on them.

I freed her, and she jumped up, her head darting everywhere.

'You're not one of them,' she said.

My hip ached as I stood. 'One of who?'

Fear possessed her face. 'The invaders.' She grabbed my

hand and dragged me to the top of the hill. Then I saw what she meant.

Several bodies were impaled on stakes, while others lay in ditches across the battlefield. The fighting continued at close quarters, hand to hand, with no mercy given. The screams and shouts hurt my ears. Blood-curdling howls covered the land like a blanket. The clash of weapons accompanied the sounds of death — swords, axes, knives and spears cut into flesh and bone and turned the earth red. In the sky, hundreds of arrows were released from either side, flying through the air before landing, piercing eyes, necks, chests, arms and legs. Warriors slashed and stabbed at each other. I saw one man disembowelled with a pole, his shit cascading out of him and stinking the air. Then his attacker was decapitated by a giant scythe, his head bouncing over the ground and landing at my feet. Blood oozed through the land, drawing in the rats and vultures swooping above. A man stumbled past, missing the lower part of his face as he tried to speak without his jaw. He reached for the girl, but I knocked him out of the way.

'Is there somewhere safe?' I said.

She pointed to a neighbouring hill and the castle on top of it. 'Only there.'

A volley of arrows landed nearby, and the screams grew closer.

'Okay,' I said. 'Run ahead of me.'

She didn't need another prompt, speeding off like a hare with its tail on fire. I ran by her side, steadying my pace. All my troubles, my worries for Diana, got shoved into the shadows as I focused on getting the girl safe. My chest ached as I took great strides to get up the hill, seeing that the battle had already reached this far.

The fields around the castle were blood red, piled high

with corpses as if they were crops ready to be harvested. As they danced in and out of the surrounding feast, vultures flew everywhere, thick in number. The sun split its rays across the land, its deep hue so red it turned the ground below it from a fervent green into corpse red. The sky was no longer blue but as crimson as a severed throat, the clouds hanging there like the internal organs of a condemned man. The girl peered at this fearful sight, her whole body shrinking as if it was a sign from the gods – a symbol of our impending punishment.

'What's your name?' I said to her.

'Jacinda,' she replied.

'Do you have family in the castle, Jacinda?'

Darkness covered her face. 'My mother and older sister.'

I took her hand. 'Let's get you back to them, then.'

We ran to the gates, a sudden fear flowing through me that they wouldn't let us in. But Jacinda waved to the guards on the walls, and they opened up. The great wooden barrier creaked open, and the girl dragged me inside. The few guards were outnumbered by two dozen weary-looking men, women, and children. A tall, thin teenage girl peeled away from the others and ran towards us.

'Jacinda!' she shouted.

I let the girl go to her sister and took stock of the situation. The data communicator had selected a random planet and point in history to keep as much distance in time and space between the Watchers and me, but I didn't know what to do next. I found an empty spot in the courtyard and sat, resting my back against a barrel. A catalogue of grim faces surrounded me, but they were too busy worrying about events beyond the walls to take notice of me.

Inside the castle, the smell of lavender lingered everywhere, drifting off the numerous flowers clinging to the walls. Water flowed from a fountain in the centre of the courtyard, its natural effervescence contrasting with the dour faces of the guards keeping watch on every person there.

Flaming arrows flew over our heads as I removed my bag and peered inside it to study what I'd gained from two years with the Watchers: mini data communicators and a spare Time Ring. I withdrew the Ring and slipped it into my jacket pocket, hoping it would be safe there.

Then I took a deep breath and gathered my thoughts. Should I return to the library for Diana even though she told me not to? I gazed at the marks on my wrists, still with no idea how they'd got there, the same with the one on my back. Diana had said she'd explain what they were, but everything went to Hell so quickly she never had the time.

So there I was, on a medieval planet, with no idea what to do next. Then the kid helped me out.

'Are you hungry?' Jacinda said.

I couldn't remember the last time I ate, but my stomach rumbled to tell me something was wrong. And my throat was as dry as sand.

'Yes, thank you.'

She smiled at me. 'This is my sister, Magda. Our mother is in the castle, helping feed the villagers who fled here for safety.'

I got up and went with them. We strode through the courtyard, under an archway, and into the interior. Flickering torches added light to the internal gloom, the flames doing their best to erase the chill in the air. Damaged weapons lined the walls, trophies from battles won, some still with blood staining their metal. A group, mainly women and children, were gathered around a set of tables in the centre of the room. Jacinda peeled away from us and ran to them, hugging an older woman I assumed was her mother.

'Are you an outlander?' Magda said to me.

I glanced at my clothes compared to theirs, chastising myself for not checking where Deminaur was on technological advancement. Yet, when studying her, I guessed her use of the term outlander didn't mean somebody off-world. But perhaps she thought I was with those who had invaded her land. And if she felt like that, then so might some of the miserable-looking guards peering at me. My guts rumbled again as two armed men walked towards me. I considered making a diplomatic exit when something large crashed through the roof.

'Fire!' somebody shouted as flames burst through the falling debris.

A small boy with a twisted, malformed back ran past me. A grey monkey with blazing red eyes sat on one of his shoulders as a surge of flame swept through the wooden wall, leaping from curtain to curtain, devouring canvases and jumping to the carpet. People screamed and fled from the fire towards me. But some weren't quick enough, and the flames leapt onto their backs before they could escape, bursting from them as if they were wearing fiery red cloaks. I grabbed a shield from the floor, thrusting it up so burning people bounced off me. I stumbled to the side, watching as the inferno spread across the ivy in the rafters and consumed the roof. Bits fell around me as I jerked the shield up, the smoke billowing everywhere. I coughed violently, turning and searching for Jacinda and her family.

But they and the rest were gone, replaced by a furnace rushing towards me.

I pressed the trigger in my head.

Chapter 17

The Sins of Time

I reappeared in the hospital, standing over a man covered in tubes and with enough breathing apparatus to put a human on the Moon. If he woke at that point, I could imagine he'd think death had come for him. The sorrow I felt for this stranger masked my awareness of another presence in the room.

'You'll get us all killed.'

The voice chilled the new scar on the back of my spine. I recognised it from somewhere but couldn't remember where. As I turned, she sat in the far corner, using the shadows as a comfort blanket. Even without the familiar Ring on her finger, I would have known what she was.

'You're a Watcher?'

'I see you've fallen into blasphemous ways. Have they recruited you yet?'

'I don't know what you're talking about.'

The room smelled antiseptic, and a cool breeze blew in through the open window. My arms stretched down my sides; hands turned into fists as the tension rippled through them. If this woman was a threat, I was ready for her. There would be no running away. The device attached to my spine had given me renewed strength in my body and mind.

She leant forward. Harsh scars crisscrossed both her palms. 'Only the outcasts have followed the wrong path. The rest of us are trying to stop the likes of you from destroying everything.'

I ignored her confused words. 'How did you know I'd be here?'

I was sick of people knowing where I'd be before I did. Then, she laughed so loud that I expected her to wake the patient. Instead, the pride and frustration swept out of her.

'Didn't Diana teach you anything important? Two years she had you, and this is what you've become. The Watchers observe and record all of time and space; that's what we do.'

The bloke slept behind me as I dug my nails into my palms.

'So you know how this will play out and what I'll do next?'

I never got the chance to be a Watcher, but I'd always known how frustrating it would be to sit on the sidelines and do nothing when people needed help. My field trips with Diana watching others suffer and die had taught me that. That's why I'd done so much after escaping from them.

She rubbed at the scars on her hands and sighed. 'I wish it were so, but it's not that easy. You and your feline friend have made so many changes, and everything is in flux now. This is only one of several places you might have visited. My colleagues are at the others.'

Hugh Little coughed and mumbled something in his sleep. Even though I was there to do that, I felt guilty about waking him. But I had to get rid of this woman first. Once I'd quizzed her.

I moved forward. 'Do you know Gloriana?'

She shivered in the chair. 'We never speak about blasphemers.'

She went to cross her chest but stroked her scars instead. I was close enough to touch her, smelling lavender and rosewater on her skin. And to see the Time Ring on her finger.

'Who is Gloriana to you?'

She touched the top of the Ring. 'She isn't important now; only you are, Ruby Quartz.'

I got a clear look at her face. She looked like the silent movie star Louise Brooks, with sculpted cheeks and a black bobbed haircut. Apart from the fact her pupils were of different shapes and colours. And they shimmered and swirled like distant stars in constant movement.

'What do you want from me?'

She stopped touching the Ring, and I thought I saw it move.

'Stop meddling in things you shouldn't. That's all I can tell you.'

The slight flicker of her eyes told me she was about to leave, but I wasn't finished with her. I grabbed her wrist and turned it towards me: she had no marks there. Fear and confusion crossed her face, wondering what was stopping her from disappearing. It was a surprise to me as well.

'Now, this is unexpected,' I said as she struggled in my grip. 'Did you know about this possibility?' The croak in her voice and panic in those strange eyes told me she didn't. 'I could keep you with me forever.'

Her lips trembled. 'You wouldn't.'

'Do you know where Diana is?'

'No. The Queens took her with them.'

'Do you know where they are, what they want?'

She was scared, confused by how I'd turned the tables on her.

'Nobody knows where they are,' she stammered. 'And they want the same as you.'

'What?'

'They want to live forever, break all the laws of science and nature, and be gods of the universe and time. So you and they will destroy all of us.'

She quit fighting against me, resigned to some terrible fate she thought I had in store for her.

'I don't want to live forever.'

I let go of her hand, expecting her to disappear, but she sat and looked bewildered.

'Then what do you want?'

'What I've always wanted: to save people, and you can't do that by sitting on the sidelines making notes.'

'You're changing history, altering time and the natural order of things. You should observe and record, that's all. Isn't that what Diana taught you?'

I nodded. 'Amongst other things. She also taught me how to be kind and good, help the helpless and improve the lives of others. How does recording history do any of that?'

'All civilisations, regardless of what species they are, learn from the mistakes of the past.'

This time, I laughed out loud. 'Are all Watchers this naïve?'

'We are not gods. You and the Queens of Heaven,' she shivered as she said the name, 'are blasphemers who will destroy everything. You're an infection that needs a panacea.'

'And there's the irony – you can only watch and observe, unwilling to do anything about this terrible doom you're predicting.'

Now I knew why the Watchers had never come after me. They were incapable of changing anything, even me. And it wasn't them I'd escaped from, but the Queens of Heaven.

'It's not too late to stop,' she said. 'Not too late to save the mother and child.'

'What?'

She vanished as I reached for her.

'Have I died and gone to heaven?' the voice behind me said.

I turned around to grant him one last wish.

* * *

'These Watchers must be stalking you,' Daisy said when I returned to base and told them what had happened. It was disconcerting to see the maturity of the kid.

Dash looked concerned. 'You don't know who she was?'

'I've never seen her before in my long life.'

'Maybe she was the real Louise Brooks?'

'Wow,' I said. 'I never even thought of that.' The idea excited me. 'I would have stroked her hand more if I had.'

'So, what happened to the patient?'

'It worked,' I said. 'All I had to do was touch him, and he travelled with me. I need to try it with more people, see how many I can take.'

The possibilities were endless. Looking at Dash, I wondered if she'd thought about them.

'Was he happy visiting his grandchildren?' Lucy said.

I lifted my hand to my face and laughed. 'Once I told him what I could do, he didn't want to see them, said he didn't even like his kids, never mind any other offspring.' His language had been choicer than that, but I didn't repeat it in front of Daisy. 'We went on a whistle-stop tour of planets which can sustain human life. He was a big fan of Endora and its sentient fish and wanted me to leave him at a watering hole in Presopia.'

'Isn't that the place with the topless bar staff?' Dash said.

'Yep, it's very 1980s. He said it reminded him of his youth.'

'I'm hungry!' Daisy shouted as she chased something invisible around the room. The kid was like a plague of locusts where food was concerned.

'Let's get something sorted for us all,' I said.

Dash picked Daisy up and they danced across the base.

Lucy sidled up to me as her daughter boogied with a six-foot-tall talking cat.

'What you did was kind.'

'Don't you find any of this bizarre?' I said to her.

She removed the bow from the back of her head, letting down her long hair.

'I'm the youngest of six kids, brought up with nothing and encouraged to do nothing. I married the first man who claimed he loved me, and I endured ten years of torment to protect what I care about the most in the world. I died, and from what Dash told me, so did Daisy. So no, I find none of this strange. On the contrary, I think it's wonderful.' Her smile filled the room.

'Daisy's had no problems sleeping?'

No matter how clever the kid was, some of what she'd seen must be bothering her. From how she shaped her lips, I guessed Lucy wanted to say no before something changed her mind.

'Sometimes she talks in her sleep about being taken by that woman and...' she stared at Daisy dancing with Dash, both of us grinning at the kid's big, beaming face.

'What else, Lucy?'

Her mouth quivered as she spoke. 'Now and again, she wakes up in a sweat, saying she remembers being dead.'

It was a worrying thought that made me want to get them away from me and to safety, but how could I after she said they were so happy with us?

'Have you considered where you'll live, Lucy?' Her eyes sparkled. 'Only on this planet, though.'

She crumpled with disappointment. 'We can't stay with you?'

'What we're about to do will be dangerous to be around; you need to get Daisy somewhere safe.'

'We both feel safe here.'

'Everything they need is here.'

Dash cleaned the cutlery as she joined us. Daisy was laying the plates on the table, which now looked like it would have the pleasure of hosting its first group meal in a few thousand years.

I stared at Lucy and her daughter. 'You wouldn't be able to go up top without Dash or me.'

I imagined Daisy crawling out of the lift and scaring the tourists.

'There's a load to do here.' Daisy jumped into her mother's arms. 'There are heaps of books and stuff to read and toys, and Dash said I could play games against these super-computers.'

'Okay,' I said. 'I'll think about it while we eat.'

I'd let them stay, but I didn't want the kid too excited. As we ate, there was no talk of time travel or Watchers and their Queens. Dash had travelled two hundred years in the future to get a sample of Earth's best dishes. By the end, my gut was fit to burst. Daisy had found a pack of cards in my room and played some strange game with her mother.

'Loser does the washing up,' Lucy said as she dealt, and Daisy frowned at the thought.

'I'm glad you let them stay,' Dash said.

'They're safer here than anywhere else. But I don't trust Gloriana to leave them alone.' I didn't trust her to leave me alone.

'How do we find Diana?'

It seemed an impossible puzzle to crack. 'I've given this time loop thing some consideration.'

'You believe they're using that as her prison, keeping her there while she works on their experiments?'

I nodded. 'It seems the likeliest situation.'

'Why doesn't she travel out of there the first chance she gets?'

I jumped into a chair and pulled a computer screen in front of me.

'That's been puzzling me. I've searched every corner of my mind to find anything Diana told me about travelling through time and space.'

'And?'

'Do you remember me telling you there were points in time we could never visit?'

'Sure,' Dash replied. 'We can't travel to before life began or after it ends.'

'I never told you why.' I started a search on the computer as I spoke.

'I always assumed it was because there's nothing capable of sustaining life at those points.'

'Indeed. I've put together bits of things Diana mentioned and our recent experiences, and I think I know why there are restrictions on the Time Rings.' She furrowed her eyes. 'It's because of the energy expended at the evolutionary beginning of life and the end of life in the universe,' I said.

'Is this related to all life or only humanity?'

'This is another of those things Diana never got around to explaining. I assumed it's for human life since whoever created the Time Rings designed them for our DNA.'

'Didn't the Watchers create them?'

I shrugged. 'I assume so, but I have no evidence of it. However, Diana told me human evolution was essential to how the Rings connected to a traveller's thoughts when they pictured their intended destination.' I tapped the side of my head. 'It's the brain that takes us on our journeys, and that's why I had to modify the connection in the Ring to link with your DNA.' And why I'd needed that part of the brain from the dead version of Dash.

Her grimace told me she must have been thinking about that.

'Okay, but what does that have to do with the limits of how far the Time Rings will take a user?'

'It's all connected to energy, Dash. Our brains are full of it, but only because they've evolved over hundreds of thousands of years, transforming from the earliest humans to what we are now as *Homo sapiens*. The Time Rings can't reach certain points because there's too much energy at them, whether through evolution or the death of the universe. Our technology doesn't have enough oomph to break through the barrier. Do you remember on Avon when Oban said he'd examined the room after I'd time-jumped out of it?'

She nodded. 'I watched him do it. His scanners discovered an unusual amount of unknown energy at the point you'd vanished from.'

'Yes, and he surmised that this energy release affected a time traveller if they attempted to return near where they'd left. This is why my body collapsed on me when I got too close to an earlier version of myself at the train station on Avon.'

'So you think this energy release is connected to the beginning and end of life?'

'I assume so. According to what Diana taught me, all the Watchers knew about the end of the universe was that a massive explosion causes it. The same as at the birth, so we obviously can't travel to those points, but I think there are barriers also along the human evolutionary line.'

'How does this help us find Diana?'

'You wondered why she didn't leave, especially if the technology is inside her.' She nodded and tried to peer over my shoulder at the screen behind me. 'Because if you tether one of these time loops to an explosion large enough to prevent travelling through time and space, you have.....'

'A prison,' she said. 'But you would have to tether it to a place before the blast happened. And it would need to be a significant blast.'

'Correct. And that's why I'm searching for the largest

explosions recorded on this planet.' I glanced at the screen. 'It doesn't have to be an end of the universe type devastation.'

'Just end of the world stuff.' Dash pointed at the list. 'How do you create a prison inside one of these?'

We stared at the top results.

'August 9, 1945. That's where they'll be.' I had no doubts.

'Nagasaki? Why there and not Hiroshima or Chernobyl?'

I peered at the black-and-white images of the atomic mushroom consuming the sky over Nagasaki.

'This has the largest explosion. If Diana has continued her experiments, she needs somewhere stocked with enough provisions so her captors won't have to leave the loop regularly.'

'That makes sense. How do you think it works?'

Dash laid out her weapons as she spoke, the compact laser guns which would be two-hundred-year-old future anachronisms in 1940s Japan. I studied the historical documents gathered on the computer.

'I expect that outside the loop, it will be before the bomb is dropped, guarded with security the Queens have assembled for protection. The time inside the loop will begin at the precise point Fat Man explodes above Nagasaki at 11.02 local time. The guards inside will be renegade Watchers, keeping an eye on Diana to ensure she does whatever they need from her.'

Everything I said was theoretical guesswork.

'They must use a heavy-duty power source to run the thing.' Dash was right, and I had no idea what it would be. 'You think they'd risk a nuclear power source underneath an incoming atomic bomb?'

'I wouldn't put anything past them.' Not even the possibility of further destruction. 'We have to be on our guard when we're there.'

'If I were them, I'd have a small army around the building. Have you worked out which one it is yet?'

She charged the guns and ensured there were enough spare batteries while I scanned the data on the computer.

'The Mitsubishi Steel and Arms Works have the area to hide large experiments, but it seems too obvious. So I think they'll be somewhere in here.'

I pointed at the screen. Dash leant over my shoulder and stared at images of the Nagasaki Medical School and Hospital.

'That's a good choice,' she said. 'What better place to carry out experiments than in a hospital?'

We had a plan coming together, and I felt optimistic about it.

Then the lights went out, and Daisy screamed.

Chapter 18

Ishtar

The screaming stopped as I froze, unsure if I was dreaming again. Unseen knitting needles attempted to stitch the broken pieces of my brain into one.

'I thought it was time I introduced myself.'

I tumbled out of the chair and hit the floor, first with my elbow, then my knee. A platoon of tiny hammers knocked on my bones.

'Is that you, Dash?'

My lips trembled as my fingers scrambled around in the gloom before my eyes became accustomed to the half-light.

'The others aren't here.'

The voice was female and unknown to me. I scanned the room but found nobody. Invisible shards of glass stabbed at my hands as I pushed my body up. A woman with sculptured cheekbones and dark hair gazed at me.

'This is an impressive setup you have here; not as good as the one you had with us, but....'

As she turned, I recognised that face from Ursula's memory.

'Ishtar.' I placed a hand on my chest to stop my heart from bursting.

'Of course. I don't need to introduce myself, do I?'

'How did you find us here?'

All I thought about was the safety of the others as I searched for more intruders. No one else was in the room, not even Dash, Daisy, or Lucy. Ishtar sat opposite me and got comfortable, dropping bits of grain to the floor. She pulled a date from her pocket and bit into it, juice dribbling down her fingers and adding to the mess she'd made.

She wiped the stain from her lips with her arm. 'We're not where you think you are.'

My mind was in a fog, even more than I realised, struggling to understand what was happening. Ishtar laughed and tapped her head.

I blurted out the words. 'You're inside my brain?'

She smiled and nodded. 'I thought it best to visit you, Ruby.'

'How is this possible?'

A sickness invaded my heart, reached down into my gut and twisted away like knives in a tumble dryer.

'The communicator device you got from our friends on Kaladan; surely you knew it allows for two-way communication for anybody who has it? No? You should always check the small print of every purchase.'

I collapsed into the chair, clasping at my temple to shake her from my skull. When that didn't work, I tried to turn this strange encounter to my benefit.

'What do you want?'

Her smile vanished, replaced with a scowl. 'You need to stop what you're doing before you ruin everything.'

I was getting sick of others telling me what to do. 'You want me to quit saving people?'

She shook her head. 'Saving people is all relative. A change that benefits one could hurt thousands of others.'

There was anger in her voice as she glared at me. I needed to use that to my advantage.

'If I see someone in trouble, I will help them, no matter when or where that is.'

Defiance flooded out of me, wrapped up in a cocoon of irritation at being invaded like this.

'You're not a god, so stop playing at one.'

The heat of exploding stars radiated out of her. To her, I was nothing but a child to be chastised.

'And you are? Did you create the legend of Ishtar with your travels through time, or are you using the name to bolster your ego?'

She threw the fruit to the floor and ran long fingers into her dark hair. She wasn't dressed like a Babylonia goddess, instead wearing a pin-striped suit that wouldn't have looked out of place in a bank. She peered at me through shimmering eyes.

'We were content to observe time, watch over it and record the events of human history.' Her voice had a seductive lilt that disarmed me. I relaxed against my will. 'There may have been times when my sisters and I did things the locals perceived as godlike, but none were ever intentional.' Her gaze pierced my soul. 'Unlike your actions and that talking cat, once the two of you ripped through the fabric of time, we had no choice but to repair all the damage you've created.'

I glared at her. 'You could have stopped us.'

She removed a phone from her pocket, glanced at the screen, and turned her dismissive eyes back to me.

'We've allowed you your little dalliances, but it's time to stop that and remember who you are. Gloriana has got you marching to her dance, and if you follow her tune, you'll destroy everything.'

I struggled to understand her, worried about where my friends were and wondered what danger I was in.

'Why did you cast Gloriana out? Why do you hate her so much?'

Ishtar sighed. 'I wish I could tell you, but there are always rules about these things. But, I will say that Gloriana, for her own reasons, grew more extreme as the years went by. Now she doesn't just want to change time; she wants to recreate it in her image. And you're helping her to do that.'

I laughed at her. 'That's funny because she told me the same things about you and the Queens of Heaven.'

She dismissed my words with a flick of her hands. 'She lies.'

'Again, she said the same about you. And she hasn't been the only woman to warn me about you and the Queens. Do you know someone who looks like Louise Brooks?'

I assumed she knew who that was.

Ishtar grinned at me. 'Yes – Louise Brooks. And the thousands of lookalikes through time and space.'

'Space? There are Louise Brooks lookalikes on other planets?'

'Child, you know so little of the universe. Humans have been beaming broadcasts into space since they discovered the technology. There's a whole planet in the Tau Ceti star system dedicated to Ms Brooks. They make the most divine cocktails.' Her grin grew wider. 'Though you're far too young for anything like that.'

Her condescending tone irritated me. It was my turn to be angry, but I kept my voice under control even though my blood boiled.

'The Louise Brooks lookalike I met had scars across her hands. And she said you and the Queens were blasphemous, an infection that needed eradicating.'

'And what did she say about you?'

I took a deep breath. 'About the same.'

'Indeed.'

A volcano erupted inside me, burning through my veins as I struggled to keep control.

'I'm nothing like you, the Watchers, or the Queens of Heaven. You were the ones who stole my memories, who stole me from my parents against my will.'

My fingers dug into the sofa, teeth crunching against each other. Ishtar had invaded my mind, but I could hurt her if I grabbed her, just like the events when I was inside Ursula's mind. Or she could hurt me.

She shook her head and leant forward. 'That was your own doing, Queen of Time.'

'Wha... what?' I nearly fell onto the floor again.

She laughed at me. 'It is such a grandiose title, even for the woman who made the greatest discovery in the universe.'

She removed three small pencils from her pocket,

rolling them between her fingers as I sat there dumb-founded. Maybe this was all a nightmare, and I'd wake up soon.

'What are you talking about?'

'It was you who discovered the secret of travelling through time and space. You learned that hidden inside female DNA is the biological switch for taking the greatest journeys.'

She stared at me, waiting for a response, but I was numb. She laid the pencils on the floor in a line.

'You're mad.' I accused her of insanity, yet I felt like I'd lost my mind.

She flexed her arms and smiled. 'We think of moving through space by going from one point to another, from A to B, but you believed differently. Your theory of parallel spatial movement revolutionised travel on this planet, but what you discovered with it changed the whole fabric of space and time.' She moved the pencils so they didn't line up anymore. 'Past, present and future. Most people believed the past was gone from us and the future was something we waited for, but you thought otherwise. You believed every-thing existed at once. This is how time works.' She placed the pencils side by side. 'Once you theorised this, you assumed it must be possible to travel between these points, hopping on and off like tourists on a bus.'

'That's what the Time Rings are for.'

I believed nothing she said, but the more she spoke, the more helpful it was for me.

Shaking her head and grinning was a skill she was good at.

'No, the Rings are only facades, symbols to help the girls focus their minds on what they need to do to travel through space and time. You either have the ability inside you, or you don't. What you did with the creature from Felineous is remarkable.' She stopped talking and played with the pencils on the floor, rolling them into each other as the insides of my mind throbbed. 'I'm guessing Diana planted that little trick in your head.'

'You stole my childhood.' It was the only thing my feverish brain could think of.

'No, you did, literally. And now you don't want the rest of us to be like you.'

The pounding increased inside my brain, and I wanted to claw the Kaladan device from my skull.

'You're full of lies.' I spat the words at her. Her face was unmoving, a penetrating gaze carved in stone.

'You were fifty-six years old when you made your discovery. I remember how you railed against the universe to show you such beauty and then placed it outside your grasp.' I wanted to wake up, digging my nails into my arms until the blood dripped onto the floor. 'But you used one of your experiments to break through time and pulled a younger version of yourself from somewhere else; you and Diana railing against nature.'

'That's impossible.'

But was it?

Fragments.

'We don't know how you discovered the secret of harvesting the time energy in the brain into an external power source, but Diana will tell us, eventually.'

She got out of the chair and stamped on the pencils, shattering them into dozens of pieces as my mind was about to split into a thousand shards.

'This is more duplicity and camouflage.'

'It's only now, some years later, that I can appreciate the

irony of being able to witness all of time but not see the betrayal of my sister when it was right in front of me.'

'Your sister?' A crescendo of agony erupted behind my eyeballs.

'Yes, my sister. Diana is my sister.' My heart slammed against my chest. 'And both of us are your granddaughters.'

I was frozen in the seat when Ishtar walked over and placed her hand on my cheek before it all went dark.

* * *

I awoke to find Daisy touching my face.

'Are you okay, Ruby? I didn't mean to frighten you when I screamed. I was just excited when Mum said we could live here with you and Dash.'

'It's all right, Daisy. I think Ruby is only tired from her recent excursions.'

Dash handed me a drink of water. I scowled as I took it from her. The flutter of her eyelids told me there was more than water in the glass. I sipped at it and let the taste warm my throat.

Was it exhaustion, and had I imagined the conversation with Ishtar?

Perhaps it was a remnant from my last trip inside Ursula's mind. It might have been her memory, and I'd replaced her with myself in the dream. Was she the one who'd discovered the secret of time travel?

I ruffled the kid's hair, stood unsteadily, and grabbed Dash to stop me from toppling over. I stared at the floor and searched for the grain Ishtar had scattered.

It wasn't there.

'Come, Ruby, let's get you to bed.'

I didn't protest as Dash pulled me from the kid and

towards my room. Once inside, I sat and downed the rest of the drink.

Dash scrutinised me. 'So, tell me what happened out there.'

'How long was I out for?'

'You fainted, but it was only for two minutes. It was enough time to mumble in your sleep and keep repeating one name.'

'Which was?'

'Ishtar.'

Of course it was. I got up and grabbed the first bottle of booze I found. I poured both of us a drink.

'You'll need this.' I handed it to Dash.

Then I told her everything that had happened inside my mind.

'You don't think it was all a hallucination brought on by stress?'

She was already onto her second drink while I nursed mine.

'No, she was there. Her presence is in my head like a bruise.'

'Do you believe anything she said?'

I flopped back onto the bed and gazed at the ceiling. If I closed my eyes, what would I see there?

'Do I believe Ishtar is Diana's sister and somehow I'm their grandmother who discovered time travel and my meddling has caused so many splinters, so many fragments, that all of space and time is in danger of collapsing in on itself?'

It sounded even more preposterous when I said it out loud.

Dash didn't reply as I drifted off to sleep.

* * *

I expected to be plagued by nightmares, visions, or terrible memories, but there was nothing but inky darkness and a good eight hours of respite. Dash brought me breakfast in bed and watched as I crunched the toast in.

'Are we still going to rescue Diana?' she said.

'We are.'

'So, what's the plan for Nagasaki?'

I picked a piece of bread from my teeth and slurped orange juice.

'There's something else I have to do first.'

'What's that?'

I touched my forehead. 'I need to get this communicator out of my brain. I can't have Ishtar or anybody else pop up there whenever they want.'

'You're going into space then, and I can't talk you out of it?'

She picked up the tray from my bed. I crawled out of it and stroked her arm.

'It has to be done before we go to Japan.'

I imagined the scene of the two of us inside a nuclear time bubble sitting below the blast of an atomic bomb as Ishtar revisited my mind to distract me with more lies.

'You look after Daisy and her mom. I'll be back before you've washed those dishes.'

She curled her lips as I picked out the clothes for my trip off-world. The red boots would be perfect for the journey, shiny and bright. They would be just right for the Gleaming Planet, the place that hated me and the civilisation that would conquer Earth five hundred years in the future.

I had to go to Kaladan.

Thank You!

Thank you, dear reader for purchasing this book.

Many thanks to my wonderful wife for all her support and patience.

Extra special thanks to Karina Gallagher for being a dedicated reader of my work.

Cover design by James, GoOnWrite.com

About the Author

Andrew French lives amongst faded seaside glamour on the North East coast of England. He likes gin and cats but not together, new music and old movies, curry and ice cream. Slow bike rides and long walks to the pub are his usual exercise, as well as flicking through the pages of good books and the memoirs of bad people.

Find out more at www.andrewsfrench.com

Facebook:

https://www.facebook.com/A-S-French-Author-1501456250060018

Twitter:

www.twitter.com/andrewfrench100

Instagram:

www.instagram.com/andrewfrench100

And replies to all his email at mail@andrewsfrench.com

If you have the time, please leave a review at Amazon or Goodreads

Thank you!